Buckhead

To Verna

GRACE
The Mystical Caribbean Mission

Hope the Caribbean
adventure in this book
takes you to your very
own vibe. Enjoy the
ride ...   love

G.

GRACE
The Mystical Caribbean Mission

Geneviève Douyon Flambert

iUniverse, Inc.
New York   Bloomington

iUniverse books may be ordered through booksellers or by contacting:

iUniverse
1663 Liberty Drive
Bloomington, IN 47403
www.iuniverse.com
1-800-Authors (1-800-288-4677)

Because of the dynamic nature of the Internet, any Web addresses or links contained in this book may have changed since publication and may no longer be valid. The views expressed in this work are solely those of the author and do not necessarily reflect the views of the publisher, and the publisher hereby disclaims any responsibility for them.

ISBN: 978-0-595-51639-1 (sc)
ISBN: 978-0-595-50709-2 (dj)
ISBN: 978-0-595-61975-7 (ebook)

Printed in the United States of America

iUniverse rev. date: 09/21/09

"Music is prophecy: its styles and economic organization are ahead of the rest of society because it explores, much faster than material reality can, the entire range of possibilities in a given code. It makes audible the new world that will gradually become visible."

—Jacques Atalli: Noise (1977) Attali, Jacques (1977), Bruits: Essai sur l'économie politique de la musique, Paris, PUF.

ACKNOWLEDGEMENTS

I wrote this book listening to the leafy breeze whistle bird songs. I thank my family for sharing my life and growing the wings to fly my dreams.

Grace was born with the contributions of a village; some bits and bigger parts come to life in the fictional characters. It took several years to research information, develop the matrix, and write the first story and essential people always crossed my path, coincidentally. I thank God for synchronicity.

Special thanks to my four editors: Lyne, Flo, Guileine and Chad

To: Rosalen, Heza, Marie Josée, Paule, Roxane, Dominique, Maggie, Savannah, Earlene, Jai, my sisters in spirit, and my God-given sisters, I love you.

Thank you Franzou for our life of love.

1

BARON'S PLACE OF REST

"Behind the mountains are more mountains."

Grace sat unaware of the hot dusty road rolling under the car, oblivious to the island panorama that passed her blank stare. By the time she realized they had already made it to Tapion, her dad's car was easing over the top of the mountain. Like a slow-motion roller coaster ride, they plunged from the top of the high mountains down to sea level. Dead ahead lay the stunning Goave Bay, and she momentarily turned her attention to the amazing view, enjoying the contrast of the dense green vegetation against the Caribbean Ocean's palette of warm turquoise and larimar to deep dark-blue.

Traveling along this two-strip highway could be risky because of high mountains, deep precipices and many water passes that didn't have bridges. Thank goodness, Dad Boulay had a great car and, after traveling this road back and forth every summer since childhood, he knew each turn, plunge and water pass by heart.

This time, Grace was especially anxious to cover the long distance and actually reach Port Salut, their final destination. Ten water passes are between Hatuey and me, she thought. She knew he would probably be at the beach. She imagined him playing volleyball, unaware of time passing by, while she consciously absorbed the feeling of every mile that separated them. She just couldn't get him out of her head! Grace was totally looking forward to this spring break vacation at the beach and Hatuey constantly close-by.

Only recently had she lost control of her feelings. Since then, everything had been blown out of proportion; it was all happening too fast and she knew it. It all started at a boring volleyball party. She had not expected him to be interested in her and why, out of the blue, he asked her to dance was still a wonder. Had she thought of the possibility of dancing, she would have been listening to the music at least. But, she really wasn't paying attention and didn't know what song was playing, or else she wouldn't have accepted to dance reggae…

Then, Hatuey started smiling. He was such a good dancer! So, she followed his lead and did as he did. Bob Marley was singing the rub-a-dub style© and they let their bodies move to the groove. The crunchy beat took over and it became natural, even easy; she forgot that she had felt self-conscious, that she basically was not a good dancer. Then, the song was over and so was the magic. She felt ashamed, again, and didn't know what to do until he took her hand.

"Thanks, Grace" his irresistible smile swept her away;

"Thanks," she barely managed to whisper back.

The road to Port Salut sometimes left the 2-strip highway and skirted through a few small towns but, at last, the car veered on the small path that led to the vacation house. Gravel progressively made way to sand and the ride became smoother.

Upon their arrival, the ocean was light green with a hint of turquoise and it extended to the horizon where it melted into the sky. The crème colored sand spread like soft vanilla ice cream and the beach stretched as far as the eye could see. Hundreds of coconut trees lounged on the coastline, their necks swayed with the breeze and fruits dangled like earrings. Towards the left, not too deep or too far from the seashore was an island, small enough to cross on foot.

Grace remembered how great it had been to hang out there with her friend Canela the previous year; they had spent hours stretched-out on the island's white sand, soaking in the sun and enjoying its morning warmth, just like lizards. She couldn't wait to go back to catch more golden tropical sun rays.

Finally, Dad Boulay made a right and squeezed the big Citroen through the rickety iron-gate. As he entered the small front yard, he eased the car to a stop and parked to the right of the tomb, yes, a real tomb. Mr. Baron, the previous owner of this house, was buried in his front yard. His bones were put to rest in a cement burial chamber slightly bigger than a coffin and that rose four and a half feet off the ground; Mr. Baron's front yard had become "the lone couch of his ever lasting sleep."

Although it may seem strange to be buried in a residential area, in this case it really wasn't. It couldn't have happened within city limit, but this house was in Port Salut, which was countryside; the city code and the rural code of law weren't the same in this Caribbean country. Any qualms about the Baron's tomb had vanished for our vacationers last summer.

One night around this same time last year, Grace's brother, Toussaint, had come home late after a beach campfire. As usual, there were many family members, their friends, and some of their friends sleeping on every possible bed; none of the straw mats remained. He thought of the Citroen, but when he checked the car's spacious back seat, he found a warm body. So, he decided to find the only unoccupied flat surface... and that was the tomb. Toussaint Boulay was not very brave. So, when the next morning everyone saw him resting peacefully on top of the tomb, it was concluded that the old man Baron couldn't be so terrible; most were left with the sense that if Toussaint could take him on, anyone could. The cement structure had been demystified: only a benevolent soul could be wandering around that bone house.

2

DANCING TO THE BEACH

"When you loose: you win."

I love to dance. It's such a release, I just think about dancing and it makes me happy. Dancing in human bands or rarah parades is probably my favorite. I don't worry about being faceless in a crowd, my senses are intensified and I enjoy the adrenaline rush even better.

Dancing parades happen throughout the Caribbean and they've probably always been around. Instruments can be triangles, pieces of metal, bottles and metal graters, trumpets, bamboo and metal horns, and the melody is created with human voices singing more or less in harmony. This musical celebration is about ambiance and dancing although you hear stories about some secret societies that use rarah groups for magic.

It's amazing how many Caribbean people can hear the hollow call of a bamboo horn from afar; maybe, the deep repetitive solo note tugs somewhere at their sub consciousness. For some like the Boulays, saying they "hear" is incorrect. Rather, they claim their rhythmic frequencies have been genetically tuned, generation after generation, to certain acoustic vibrations; the correct stimulus just prompts response.

Usually, Jack Boulay was the first to get up to dance and the last one to sit and rest. Now, both Jack and his son were on their way out to join the fun passing our front door, and I decided to tag along; Grace fell-in close behind. By the time we reached the front gate, the thick of this group was passing by and we each dove into the human sea.

4

I was ready to follow this rarah to the end of the island if that's where it was headed. I focused on the words they were singing. It was part of a well-known reggae song by Bob Marley:

In a rub-a-dub style, in a rub-a-dub style,
In a rub-a-dub style, in a rub-a-dub style."©

In a way that seemed bizarre; I think it was the first time I listened to a rarah-playing earth-feeling reggae music, but Bob Marley was a Caribbean man. Nobody really cared what they were singing or if they understood the meaning anyway, as long as it was entertaining. We had quickly reached the beach and I saw Toussaint leave the group to meet some guys I thought I recognized.

Ahead of the crowd, Jack Boulay stood six feet tall but his aura made him seem taller. I watched him direct this dancing human serpent and lead everyone into a new song. Incredibly, the band kept the same beat as the front of the rarah taught us at the back the entire chorus. We danced and sang, learning the new song. Only after a while did I sense that Grace was no longer close and that made me uncomfortable. So, I tried to move towards her but too many people were between us and I couldn't cut through the crowd. I watched as she was pushed even further back.

A yellow light took just a nano second to register in my brain: danger! I turned against the current of people moving forward and tried to move quickly against the tide of dancers. Many people were obviously not appreciating me messing up their fun. Before I could react, and even before I realized what was happening, he was smack in front of me and had already sprayed my entire face. Whatever the liquid it was a mouthful not just saliva but, stinky, smelly and warm, mostly alcohol; I would still feel it and smell it for days. The worst part was that he didn't just spit in one spurt and get it over with; rather, he blew it out by finely pressing his lips together to spray the liquid all over my face, penetrating each pore; YUK!

My reaction was total disgust! Of course, I covered my eyes and tried to shield my whole face. Well at least it wasn't acid or he wouldn't be blowing it out of his mouth… And, I didn't feel my face burning. The crowd shoved me around but I couldn't even try to open my eyes because of the sting. I staggered, and was pushed and pulled, trying to wipe off my face with my tee shirt.

I finally found the side of the road and plopped down to regroup. Carefully wiping my face I worried about the liquid, possible germs and other effects. By the time I had regained my senses and found the nerve to try to reopen my eyes, none of my friends were around and the sun was no longer high in the sky. Well at least I wasn't blind! What in the world happened, I wondered? Where did everyone go? Why did that man spray my face? I felt disoriented with many unanswered questions. It felt like I was getting a headache, or maybe I was going to bawl out and cry; I just sat there and took more time to get myself together.

Traveling down memory lane, I started thinking about how my mom had let me come to Port Salut beach with the Boulays. The clan was composed of several interlocking parts. The base members were Toussaint, Grace and Pisket, along with Mom and Dad Boulay. Other more complicated parts fit into the picture because Dad Boulay had several sets of children with different women; of course not at the same time. Like son like father: Grandpa Miles Boulay had also fathered various Boulay families. Overall, it was difficult to say how many children they were. Every now and again, another Boulay popped up and I would meet yet another half brother, or uncle, sister or aunt; the second and third generations overlapped a bit. My friends seemed happy enough to have such an extensive family; they were comfortable with themselves and I readily accepted them as well. Plus, my parents had known the Boulay families since way back when they were school age children.

The youngest, Pisket, was closer to my age but my girl Grace was a true friend. Although she was three years older, an important bond connected us, like a sisterhood that had started with volleyball but had become more. Funny thing is we didn't play on the same team, nor did we even play in the same category. Grace was in the junior league and I was captain of the rookie team at my school, St Joseph's. I guess a sort of camaraderie grew between Grace and me at volleyball games every Friday at St Peter's College where all the championship games were played.

Experts say sound travels through acoustic space; it is simultaneous and nonlinear and resonates causing vibrations at the human core. Some conga-drum players know well how to use special sacred rhythms to send certain people into a trance. In fact, Grace had been touched and she had felt a response deeply within herself when the rarah's bamboo horn tooted; fact is, the rub-a-dub style© had done her in once before.

They were all singing, "In a rub-a-dub style, in a rub- a-dub style"© over and over again, almost like a chant. The reggae song the human band was playing had a powerful hypnotic effect on Grace. Her body was in Port Salut and she automatically responded with feet, legs, hips, body, arms, and hands. But, her mind was revisiting the dance at the volleyball party. With the rhythmic song, she connected past and present and after closing her eyes, she let the musical flow carry her away.

In a dream-like state, she saw Toussaint leave to join some friends at the beach. Not too far ahead and making his way to the front was her dad. A little hypnotized, she took time to realize the song had changed, because the words that sounded out of her mouth were not the same as those in her ears. She revisited her dance with Hatuey during the volleyball party and seeing him before her could only be part of her dream, or so she thought.

"Hi, Grace, when did you get here?" The dream had spoken. How strange! When he touched her hand, she almost jumped out of her skin:

"Easy there!" he said, and only then did she realize that he was for real. Before she could figure out what to answer, he spoke again,

"I'm glad you're here."

He looked even more handsome in the afternoon sunlight, his orange-brown skin glistening; the bridge of his nose and his cheeks had been burned terracotta red by the sun. Hatuey was over six feet tall, which is a good height for a volleyball player. You could say he was of pure Caribbean extract, which means his DNA came from various sources. At first glance, you knew he had some Indian blood, because of his dark copper skin tone and his straight, coarse, jet-black hair. But his callipygian hind muscles would suggest African ancestry. Careful examination of his lineage would reveal European contributions to his gene pool as well. Hatuey was attractive, and even more alluring was the fact that he was pre-med, a college boy and to Grace he had the charm of an older and more experienced man.

Desperately, Grace wracked her brains to find something smart to say. She wanted to sound mature and sure of herself. Before she could think of anything Hatuey asked:

"Where's your twin?" The question left her perplexed; it was not literally true because she did not really have a twin, it had to be some kind of a joke. He could only mean Canela, she thought, although there was no way they could ever pass for sisters.

Grace looked like an ebony queen: tall and long-boned, her naturally flowing movements were elegant and precise, as though she were a direct descendant of Fulani or Wolof royalty. Small and feisty, Canela's medium brown skin and short rasta curls could be found in any city in America, north, central or south, on any island in the Caribbean. However, Canela and she were always together at volleyball games and that is where she also ran into Hatuey.

She then searched the crowd for Canela, finally remembering they had been together. Her eyes scanned the area where she had last seen her girlfriend, but she was not there. She could clearly see in front of her but no one she knew was within eyesight. Grace glanced back; no one was there either. When she looked back to Hatuey, she was hoping he would still be there. Her eyes locked to his and she held his gaze to make sure he didn't disappear.

"I wonder where everyone else could be?" she said aloud. Then she remembered Toussaint catching the corner of her eye a while back, as he left the rarah to join some friends at the beach. But, she hadn't seen her dad in a while and that wasn't a reassuring discovery.

The song changed back to Rub-a-Dub© and she noticed it right away this time. Hatuey danced behind her smiling. She stopped thinking about her dad, about Canela, about being worried; she stopped thinking all together. The rarah was moving ahead happily, everybody was having a private party and the collective effect was one hell of a good time. Mixed stenches had numbed her sense of smell, her body moved to the rhythm and she took the music in through her ears and all of her pores; she was actually enjoying dancing. There were many people in the group, but there was no violence, no pushing, or pulling, everyone had a happy smile and moved along to the contagious beat. When they came to the end of the path instead of veering left to follow the road the rarah headed strait for the ocean.

The front-end of the rarah entered the sea first, people set flower-covered rafts and food in the water. Grace could see heads tied in white and blue handkerchiefs and the flowing movements of arms setting small boats to float on the water; they sang and danced waiting for the colorful flags to snap in the wind.

     ♪ *Ezili o, Ezili sa, while sailing on the sea my canoe overturned, if not for the grace of God we would not have been saved.*♪

They sang over and over. It started to get creepy and Grace wasn't too sure what to do. She looked to Hatuey for direction, his warm eyes were reassuringly sexy, and he didn't appear worried at all.

"You can do this," he danced, and drew near holding her arms outstretched from side to side,

"You can do this," he whispered convincingly in her ear their bodies joined at the hips and moving as one.

It felt as if invisible strings were pulling her from within, almost like a puppet. Her legs felt heavier and heavier. The drumbeat seemed to get louder and the pace quickened, her feet automatically shifted and moved one after the other edging her closer to the water. She lost control to a magnet located underground that connected to metal implants inside the soles of her feet, or so it seemed. The rhythmic thumps of the drums were communicating with her body and the automatic responses were beyond her control.

Grace thought the water would feel cold or at least wet... Nevertheless, when she put her foot down all she would feel was herself slide into oblivion and everything and everybody around her disappeared.

3

ON THE TRACE OF MY FRIEND GRACE

"What you don't know is greater than you."

Spooky feeling, where had the group gone? I reached the end of the widest path and didn't see anyone; didn't hear a thing either. Better go to the beach, I thought that was my best option, and started walking back.

I remembered the area more or less, because I had checked it out on a friend's small motorcycle last year. Majis he was called, and he was some kind of local area official who always came to visit Altagracia and Jack Boulay in Port Salut; Majis was an all-around good guy and everyone's friend.

Reaching the bend in the road, I saw the boulder and instantly remembered Majis' warning last year,

"This rock is called *wosh sispann*, you must avoid passing close-by, especially at night."

"What's that?" I had asked, wondering what geological era he would say it belonged to. Majis explained:

"It's been energized by a dying person's breath, so it is inhabited by a *bahkah*."

I couldn't believe my ears. A dying person energized the rock with breath and turned it into what? But Majis looked dead serious, so I didn't insist; no need to be rude when he was just trying to be friendly.

Thinking the boulder didn't look mysterious I kept walking; just a big ol' rock, I had to laugh to myself. These guys see magic everywhere, all I could see was an ordinary gray mass strategically set on the side of the road.

I strolled by wondering how full the road must have been for us to dance through without my noticing where we were back in the rarah.

"Young lady." I jumped, the voice was right behind me yet I had passed no one.

"Curly-head rasta!" I had to smile and turn around.

"I believe this is yours," she said handing me a small brown seed set in a silver circle. Her dignified and severe look was crowned with a white turban. A low-cut white cotton dress strapped her waist but let an ample skirt flow gracefully around her full-size body.

I tried to examine the small ball and kept an eye on the mysterious lady. Her features were flat and angular, like they had been cut with a machete.

"No, sorry, this doesn't belong to me,"

I answered, and I tried to hand it back to her, taking a step in her direction. She crossed her strong arms and the chipped bright red nail polish on her fingertips looked like blood against her semi-sweet chocolate skin. The woman shook her head and refused to take it back.

"I'm sure it's yours; keep it," she insisted, quickly adding "you'll need it."

Why would I need a brown seed with a silver circle? I didn't even know what it was.

"What is it?"

"The seed is a *jebourik*: it is a universal poison antidote; you just add to boiling water, let it seep, and then drink the mixture. No poison will kill you. Wear it as a pendant on a chain around your neck and it will protect you from your enemies."

Yea, ok, whatever! I took the cool-looking pendant and put it on the silver chain that was already around my neck. I could easily throw it away once I left this bizarre meeting. Since the lady was still standing in front of me, I figured maybe she was waiting to get paid. So, I tried to offer her money but she seemed rather offended.

"No, I'm not selling you the *waree* seed. I'm giving it to you."

"Why?" I was very curious about her answer.

"To make sure you are not tricked by detractors." I didn't understand who would want to trick me.

"You must have mistaken me for someone else." Her smoky black eyes burnt like hot peppers through my retina clearing a path to profound truths.

"I know what I've been told and I know what I have done. Take it, wear it, you won't regret."

She motioned for me to put it around my neck and I decided to obey, at least for the time being. To my surprise, she thanked me then thought necessary to mention that I would be seeing her again… That didn't sound like good news to my ears.

I walked more than ten minutes and was hot and dusty before I reached the hotel area. Port Salut has a cute little hotel and even an airstrip close-by for guests who prefer to travel by plane. I thought that maybe I could run into to someone I knew, so I hurried my step toward one of the entrances.

A bamboo fence surrounded the hotel property. I had heard stories of indiscreet bamboo that reveal the secrets of those who try to hide between the thin branches and leaves. I listened carefully to the breeze weaving through the pointy leaves but heard nothing, barely the bristle of warm air. Certainly no spot for a Koala bear!

Before I reached the entrance, I heard, then saw a motorcycle coming out of the driveway; I recognized the face right away. Majis made it up to me and stopped by my side.

"Hello,"

"Hello Majis how are you?"

"Hi Canela, how is it I see you here, what's wrong, you seem to be alone…"

"I was in the rarah with Grace, Mr. Boulay and others, but I got lost."

"So, what are you doing? Do you want a ride?"

"I guess so; could you drop me off at the beach?" The beach would be a central area where I was sure to find someone I knew playing volleyball.

"Thanks Majis" and I hopped onto the small motorcycle behind this character I was happy to see. The motorcycle took off slowly and Majis turned his head:

"You walked all by yourself, that's very risky, you're lucky you didn't have an encounter."

I instinctively brought my hand to my chest to touch the *jebourik* hanging from my neck… I had stopped thinking about it.

"Do you remember what I told you last year about the big rock?"

Did I remember, of course I remembered, but I wanted more information and decided to play dumb.

"What rock Majis, what are you talking about?" I could feel stiffening in his back and shoulders.

"Canela this isn't a game, what you don't understand is greater than you. After sunset you may be unaware of dangers you should never have to face. You are a city girl and don't really see everything; things you can't control happen here in the country, you have to be more careful."

My heart skipped a beat; I wanted to tell him about my meeting but thought the timing was wrong. I took a deep breath and tried to sound casual as I answered,

"Ok Majis, take me to the beach and tell me about all evil dangers I cannot see." I finished my comments with a grin he couldn't see but I could sense my words had affected him; he had registered my sarcastic tone, and probably thought I was mocking his beliefs. We rolled in an uneasy silence for a few feet that he interrupted abruptly,

"Ok ok, I'm going to tell you anyway, because I must, you do as you please. Around here, everybody knows that the rock I pointed out to you stands vigil. The landowner bought the services of a sorcerer, asking him to energize the boulder to watch over his property. At night, you can hear the sinister clinging of the chains while it covers its territory making rounds. If ever you are caught, you need to remember the words Tantinn tann tonton, because without that magical phrase you cannot be released."

Tantinn, funny that's what I called my aunt Florence and tonton was my uncle's name. OK, I was convinced and decided I would not wander in that area during the night.

What I really wanted to ask was about meeting people there and what that meant, but we were already at the beach.

"Majis, you talked about encounters, what kind of other encounters could happen there?"

"Well" he said stopping to let me off,

"Don't worry about that part… that's more complicated. Remember the silk-cotton tree, that's the limit; just don't go beyond the tree again alone, especially not at night, ok?" My curiosity and concern about the lady I had met automatically doubled.

"I'm going to try to see where that rarah was headed. I'll tell Mr. Boulay that you are on the beach."

"Ok thanks Majis," I knew I wasn't getting any more information at that time. Looking toward the ocean, I could see Toussaint and other friends playing a lively game of volleyball.

"I'll remember not to walk in that area, I believe you Majis, trust me, I believe you."

Now a little spooked, I wondered if maybe I should be worrying about my friends and the rarah. I looked at the sea line and everything looked normal, there was a volley ball game on the sand and people in the ocean were enjoying the cool water. Bah, I pushed my concerns to the back of my mind; my friends would probably be back soon tired and happy about their rarah with stories about their dancing adventures.

4

BACK TO THE FUTURE

"With patience you can see an ant's belly button."

Grace could not believe her eyes. Where in the world could this be? She concentrated on herself, feeling her feet bounce off the rocky bottom; the springy sensation was new and disturbing, like she was buoyant. Strangely enough, she had no need for oxygen; it felt like she was breathing but didn't require air coming through her nostrils. . . This was different. She  kept walking, mechanically, taking notice of her body. Although her feet seemed more or less normal, her legs, her thighs, and arms were bloated, like they were filled with air. But she wasn't swimming, no Grace felt like she was on the moon, walking in slow motion.

How bizarre! Where is this, she wondered, the Twilight Zone? Her surroundings confirmed her suspicion of being *Anbadlo*. Colorful coral reef and beautifully shaped seashells lined the bumpy path she followed; but the carefully arranged garden, with purposeful patterns, did not appear at all like the ocean bottom. Maybe I'm in an aquarium, Grace kidded herself, nervously. She was more than worried; she was close to panic. Where she could be? She tried to remember how she got there in the first place and her thoughts returned to Hatuey.

Warm, tingling feelings of his body against hers tightened her chest and tied a knot in her throat; the sensations gave meaning to her memories. She went back to the last moments, trying to recall every detail to determine when she left "there" and how or why she was here . . . wherever "here" was.

Maybe it was the rarah, she thought. An evil sect had taken me to this unknown place and left me here. But why was everybody gone? Why did I land here and not Hatuey? Were we not together? She kept moving, trying to get somewhere, anywhere that would help figure out how to get back home. Suddenly she noticed movement by her side and she switched her attention to her surroundings. Strangely, she was unable to do both, that is focus upon her thoughts and to look around simultaneously.

An oversized sea horse bobbed alongside her and went in the same general direction, its green mane flowing like the strings of torn palm leaves in the breeze. It moved progressively closer to her until they both were side by side. Neither Grace nor the seahorse looked in the other's direction. After a while, she stopped suddenly; so did the seahorse. She then took two more steps and stopped. The seahorse moved along as though it was well aware of her next move: they moved in unison. It was magical so she tried again, making her moves quicker and more complicated. Wouldn't you know seahorse was right there with her? She abruptly changed direction, moving backwards, and the seahorse floated right along with her. Frustrated, Grace began to run while the seahorse moved alongside casually. Exasperated, she stopped and turned, the seahorse doing the same until they faced the same direction. In an attempt to tame it, she lifted her leg to mount the animal. Much to her surprise, it held still, waiting patiently as she got cozy. The seat was wider and more comfortable than she had anticipated. She looked around the neck trying to find a noose or a rein to control the animal's movement, finding nothing but the full green mane. Now that she could touch it, she knew that is was made of a material similar to a torn palm leaf, but it felt softer and cotton-like rather than fibrous as she had imagined. The seahorse took off swiftly, but the ride was so surprisingly smooth that she really didn't have to hold on at all. After all, where would she be leading the animal? She had no idea where she was going.

Seahorse left the path and started winding through the algae trees with shiny crystalline flowers, alongside the coral reef decorated like Christmas trees with multi colored balls and bubbles. The paths were well marked and certainly well kept, but you had to know where you were going to get anywhere. Grace realized she would have reached nowhere plowing ahead on the path she had taken. At least now she could hope to get somewhere, seahorse seemed quite sure of the way.

They were traveling rather rapidly and it felt as though she had been sitting on its back a good long while, but seahorse wasn't slowing down. Grace wondered if she had decided wisely when she had hopped on the animal's back. How could she know right from wrong in this Never Never Land where she didn't know how to react or what to expect?

Her thoughts shifted from her immediate environment back to the rarah. Actually, she could hear the song the rarah was singing when they approached the water:

♪ *Ezili o, Ezili sa*, while on the water my boat tipped over, if not for the grace of God I would not have been saved. ♪

Maybe the song was what did her in? Why could she hear it louder and louder in her head? She started to feel the vibrating thump of drums in her chest. Once again, she felt her legs getting heavier, and the soles of her feet seemed magnetically attracted to the ground. She had the same feeling towards the end of the rarah. The seahorse slowed down and entered a gated area studded with royal palm trees; blocked passageways rose up automatically, just as the animal approached. It was certainly a well-choreographed coincidence … Finally, they cautiously entered a series of gardens and followed mazes that took them to a garden looking somewhat like one back home: rows of green shrubs carefully planted in perfect lines in reddish-brown dirt.

The seahorse came to a halt and Grace jumped off. It stood next to her, showing no sign of fatigue after the long travel and her extra weight. In a thankful gesture, Grace touched the animal's long neck; she thought she caught a wink in its eye, as if it could answer; the idea made her smile. A lively *palm chat* came to visit and chirped a storm around the seahorse's head. Grace left the two friends to their chatter and looked around trying to identify her surroundings and longed to find something, anything, familiar. Timidly, she picked a leaf from one of the small shrubs. It looked like a plant from back home; that thought sent her back to Port Salut. She wondered what had happened to her family and her friend Canela. The leaf she held was oblong and somewhat droopy, and laced in a sweet-pungent smell. Next to her a deep and smooth voice resonated,

"That's Basilicum, of its Latin name, or Sweet Basil in English. Welcome to my garden," said the lovely lady with a warm smile. Grace wasn't startled; the lady's presence was comforting, somewhat soothing, but she didn't know why. She tried hard to remember her mother's teachings, so she didn't raise her eyes and kept her voice on a level tone when she said:

"Good evening ma'am".

"Thank you for coming, my child; I'm the greeter of our world-nation and keeper of teachings from the Ancients; they recommend you cut plants at dawn, when they are still covered with dew, the best day is when the moon is in its first quarter. Always remember to ask the universe for its permission first."

After getting off Majis' motorcycle, I stood a while under a sea-grape tree and enjoyed the shade of its thick, round leaves while I tried to locate my friends. I could see Pisket in the water close to the shore, enjoying a swim alone as usual. I'm not so sure why, but I couldn't help notice that Piskit was often alone; it's as though she had a hard time relating to people. I really would have rather played volleyball than swim anyway, so I sat in the shade to check out the game.

Although I could not name of all of the players, I certainly knew most of their faces. The first one I identified was my favorite lefty, the one everyone called Bob, short for Alberto; he stood a head above the crowd. Bob was probably everybody's favorite player in the league; he was certainly among the best-looking. His most stunning feature was his deep, dark-chocolate complexion; this was complemented by a pair of shiny marble-black eyes, a winning smile, and plenty of self-assurance. Unstoppable, he was just like his smash hits in volleyball. Close–by, Joel was playing setter. Both fellows were lanky, but Joel was no more than 5'10", whereas Bob was over six feet tall. Quite the contrast, Joel was a blond haired and light-skinned Caribbean teenager. Tropical blondes are natives on just about every Caribbean island and sometimes look like Joel: a caramel rolled in sesame seeds.

Lost in my thoughts, I came back to reality when I noticed that their game had ended. My friends' team had won, they were switching sides of the court, and another team was getting ready to play against them. Although I didn't really mind playing against my friends, I certainly would have preferred to play with them. So, I decided to wait the game out, until Joel called me from under my tree.

"Canela, come and play with us, Gina is tired and wants to call it quits."

I didn't wait to hear my name called twice. I was only too happy to play volleyball with my friends. I ran up to the court smiling and waving my hand to known faces. Of course, Joel no longer wanted to play setter; I got the job, but didn't mind at all. Actually, it was my favorite position. I loved being the one to set up the play, to see the open spots in the adversary's defense and position my teammates to deliver a winner. I was the designated setter and Bob would start in the top right corner. Starting in the two back positions were Maurice and Marina, two tall and well-rounded players. Finally, front and left was a shorthaired girl who played all positions well; although she was short, she had the highest jump I had ever seen and a pretty good kill. With our rotation ready, we took position to begin.

We won the toss and the game started sluggishly. Marina went to serve, hitting a fair tennis serve that just barely went over the net. The front line of the opponent's team answered, hitting it once, the second pass to set the kill, but their player wasn't ready so they just bumped the ball back to us. Joel defended and set Bob up with a backset. Bang, smack on the 3-meter line in their court, giving them no chance to defend. Our first point was convincing but just the beginning of a series of great team efforts: ruthless on the attack and a mean defense, and let's not forget a setter with vision! Marina served seven points in a row before they broke our lead; then, they got the serve and the chance to score points.

I was still in the middle, behind Joel and waiting on the defense to set up the play. A nice smash-serve came over the net and Maurice missed the defense. 7-1. The strong serve came again, strait at Maurice (the opponent knew he had a client and would keep them coming his way). Maurice missed the second serve and hit the ball into the water, 7-2. We all faded back, bracing ourselves for the third serve, which went high up in the air and then straight into the net. Too bad!

Bob was going to serve for us. His serves were great when they landed on the court. He tossed the ball in the air with his right hand, jumped up, and smash hit it over the net. They didn't even get it off the ground. Ace in the hole: 8-2. Bob went back to serve, but was less aggressive and didn't attack the ball; the wobbly serve went over the net, but they missed the defense bump, expecting a canon ball they overreacted, 9-2. Bob served again, the other team struggled for the defense, and sent it back with a dink, a one-handed set strategically placed to fool the adversary. But Joel was right there; he bumped it to the shorthaired girl and she smashed it into their back row. They hit it straight back at us; Maurice lifted it right to me and I set Joel up for the break, a short set in the middle . . . just the way he liked 'em; Joel hit the ball with perfect timing and it landed on the other side, plunk, again our point, 10-2. We were killing them and loving every minute of it. They called for a time-out to regroup and we gathered in the center of the court.

"Ok, we're doing great, everything is being done right, let's just fight for these 5 next points and the win is ours."

We put our hands together and I said:

"Ready, aim," and everyone said in unison, "FIRE!"

We were fired up all right. Bob went to the service line again and blasted the ball that hit the opposing player before his arms were ready: 11-2. Wow, what a point! I hoped he would try that serve again, which he did. Two steps, the ball went up along with him and he hit as he was coming down, a bit late, and the ball crashed into the net; it was now their ball.

Their first serve was manageable; we defended, set, and smashed it over. They answered the same and the exchange became the most passionate of the whole game. We would each set up a good game, hit it well while the other team would defend and then counter attack; the ball went back and forth over the net six times, neither side letting up, refusing to loose the point. Bob came up with the winner from the back. I set him one up high, right behind the three-meter line and he jumped up with all of his six feet and some inches and came down

on the ball with a roar. I don't know what startled them more; the strength of the hit or the sound made by the player, regardless, the opponent's team was unable to control the ball.

Joel to serve, which was good, he hit it square, with his palm flat and the ball went over floating. Joel's first serve zigzagged and dropped on the court before anybody on the other side realized what had happened; 12-2 was the score now. Players lined up on the side of the court ready to play the next game. They were teasing the losing team, to make them lose concentration and continue their losing streak, and that's just what happened. I never got my chance at the net, the game ended after Joel's four serves in a row, the final score15-2.

I had a quick thought for my lost friends but didn't have the time for lengthy concern. We had to play again. New players were ready on the other court, so we quickly decided to stay in the same rotation. Winner gets the ball, ours was the serve, and Joel was our man. That's how we started the second game.

5

AN ISLAND GIRL'S EDUCATION

"Mice are always born with a tail."

Grace politely listened to her host as she explained:

"The leaf you're touching, the Sweet Basil, was used in Egypt to embalm cadavers when preparing mummies. Mummies like many other things that you will learn in this world-nation seem ancient, because we are the keepers of the beginnings. From now own you must pay close attention because it's up to you discern how your discoveries here relate to you, specifically."

Grace quietly observed the lady before her. She was tall and wore a long white Greek-like toga or robe. Her short, fuzzy, cinnamon-brown hair matched her terra-cotta skin. The only feature you really noticed were the pair of avocado eyes that drew you in, capturing your gaze in the cool stillness of wells untouched by time.

"Ayizan is what I am called; I am the first station because I greet visitors and I also bless them and purify their energy so that they may proceed on their journey. Who may I ask are you?"

"My name is Grace Boulay, I don't know where I am, how I got to this world, or why I'm here in front of you."

Ayizan looked at Grace with a sympathetic smile.

"Sorry to say, I don't know why you are in front of me either. I don't know anything about you, but I can tell you about where you are now. This place is without time, a concept that is the most difficult for visitors to accept. The easiest way I can explain is to put it this way: here there are no seconds,

20

no minutes, no hours, no days, no weeks, no months, no years. This is the world-nation of those who keep the essence of creation's beginnings. I may be your first encounter with the *lwa*, the keepers, but there are many others, each the gate master of a world-nation.

What you see with your eyes is the product of our energies reflected upon your retina, filtered through your perceptions, interpreted through your cultural representations, and received through the channels of your personality. It's our world-nation but your surroundings are unique; I see a totally different place, so this place is apparently different but essentially the same for everyone. It all depends upon the eye of the beholder. Your journey here has either three or seven steps that you must complete. How you proceed and how quickly you learn to move on to the next level is your choice."

Grace thought about what Ayizan explained and tried to pick out the key information.

"I would really like to take the three-step journey, if I may ..." She said, trying to sound as respectful as possible.

"Ah my child, if that's what you want then I sure hope that's what you'll get." That sounded more promising than anything she had heard so far, so Grace insisted:

"Please help me, what should I do to get there?" Ayizan was more than willing to inform her; sparks of light shot from the large silver hoops that dangled from her ears and framed her heart-shaped face.

"Well, ok. The first thing you must know is a proper greeting. I've noticed many young people don't have the good manners to utter a simple 'Hello,' though around here, it's a little bit more complicated.

You will need to give a proper greeting each time to get your foot through the door of every level you must complete. A lwa, controls each entrance, and serves as the guardian, the ruler, the spirit and the mystery of that world-nation. To greet a lwa you shake both hands, right then left, then your forearms form a cross, after which you slowly spin around three times,—twice counter-clockwise, first and last, and in between once clock-wise—finally you bow or curtsey."

Grace tried but was unable to remember the sequence immediately and that presented a problem. She absolutely had to learn this greeting to move on. She cursed her lack of ability, feeling frustrated, especially because her dad was such a good dancer. If she could just accept the idea of a special greeting, it would probably be easier for her to learn it. So she kept trying, practicing and practicing. Ayizan turned her around and around, laughing and acting silly while Grace began to feel dizzy. After a while, though, she started to relax and it finally clicked; the sequence became crystal-clear in her head. She instinctively found her new friend's right hand, then the left, and she no longer resisted the turning to the left, then right, then left again. Her body memorized how to set her right foot slightly aside and then to the back, and soon enough she was even imitating Ayizan, gracefully tilting her head to the right.

Once she had let go of her reservation and had practiced the movements long enough they seemed second nature, she allowed herself be drawn into the sequence of the formal greeting; her body instinctively anticipated and went through the motions.

"I think I've got it, I can do it!" Grace said happily. "Can I move on, oh please let me go to the next level Mistress Ayizan, I won't forget what you taught me, I promise."

Ayizan's melodious voice seemed to echo:

"Life-lessons are meant to be remembered and you will need the knowledge to build upon and move on; forgetting will cause you to repeat the cycle. You have gained entry to my nation and you have properly greeted me, now I must continue my work with you. Your purification will take place under the royal palm. Like the gum tree, this tree is one of my emblems and you are sure to find me there, would you need me; if I'm not in my basil garden, of course," Ayizan said, winking her left eye.

"Look toward the east for a royal palm tree, my majestic friend fluttering its leaves and caressing the wind; you will recognize it by a spear, its steeple, poking the sky; that is where I connect best with the eternal world. And that is where we shall meet."

Grace looked in the direction she pointed and saw the tall royal palm in the distance; she wondered what might be between here and there, feeling pushed out of her comfort zone. The joy brought on by mastering the greeting dropped flat, her confidence level taking a dive.

"How . . . um . . . Are we going together?" The ageless entity felt her despair,

"Don't worry, I have some things to collect to bring along; you can go with Vélékété, my trusted companion who brought you here, I'm sure he knows the way. Go fearlessly my child, it is important for you to control your fear; wicked ones feed on fear and evil thoughts." Ayizan put her arm around Grace's shoulders, gave her a hug, and leaned her chin on the girl's short hair,

"Trust in yourself and in your destiny my child, you have done well so far. I will serve you as long as your cause is just, if not you will become my enemy." Then she gently shoved her off towards the designated tree, turned around and was on her way.

Grace started walking slowly in the direction of the royal palm tree, figuring Vélékété would show up eventually. Since she was in a hurry to move on to return to her reality, she chose to start to walk rather than wait.

She could see the palm tree from a distance and it was easy to walk in the right direction. Her bloated body stood above her tiny feet and she swayed along the path that seemed to lead in the right direction; she guesstimated it shouldn't take more than fifteen earth minutes to get there. Minutes, she thought, were a guaranteed measure she could count on back home. How she yearned to be with her family and friends! She really missed her normal life. Her strides became longer, as she was now more accustomed to the conditions and that allowed her to move more quickly. Funny, she realized, walking here was fun. The path curled up toward a gathering of shapes and colors. Vivid orange stalks topped with shiny orange balls stood out and caught her attention because orange was Canella's favorite color. Surrounding the orange stalks were yellow pointy tuber shapes that ended with sinewy branches. Light-green patches on reddish-orange underground filled the lower spaces, and the floor-bed looked just like earth moss. Luminescent eels darted in and out of a batch of deep-red coral tubes . . . They seemed to be the only animal life so far, Grace realized, besides Vélékété and his bird friend, of course. Where was it, anyway? She looked at the tall majestic palm and it seemed to move closer, thrusting up just behind the small hill.

Grace soldiered on, thinking about food for the first time since her arrival in this world-nation. She wasn't really hungry, but it had been a while since she last had food, so, if only by habit, she wondered where she could get her next meal. White rice and shrimp, she could just taste it in her mouth. What were her chances of getting a good meal in this place? Slim to none she figured. She was quickly approaching her destination and could see from a distance that she would not be alone.

A gathering of people dressed in white stood around and sat casually close to the palm tree. Grace slowed her pace and took shorter steps. She had relaxed during this walk but now her heart was pounding again. She wondered what these people were going to do, and how she would participate. Since they were awaiting her arrival, they took notice as she approached the group. Grace felt self-conscious about her appearance, especially since it seemed that everyone knew about her. She reluctantly joined the crowd, feeling apprehensive about the situation and events about to take place.

Suddenly, a deep, clear voice called out. The masculine voice sang notes that she knew. but she couldn't understand the words he was saying. The crowd formed a chorus as it gathered around the palm-tree. The first song ended and the song-master led the group in another. Grace could follow this one better; it was in her native language. They were singing about opening the gates for an old man called Legba and the group would join in the chorus,

"*Papa Legba, k'ap e pase e e la veye zo,*" *a cappella*, voices in harmony: alto, soprano, and baritone carried the melody. Grace saw her friend, Ayizan, emerge from behind the tree, like she had been there all the time, only invisible, cloaked until the moment was right. She had grown old and her ageless voice resounded very slowly:

"Invested with the powers of mambo *Ayizan Vélékété, négresse mamou, ladée négresse Fréda Dahomey, négresse fredassy Fréda, négresse flavoum fréda, négresse cissafleur Vodoun da Guinen, kanjole sousafleur Vodu dagimen.*"

Grace tried to get lost in the crowd. Everybody had joined in the singing and she listened to the parts she could understand. Feeling more comfortable, she raised her head to look around. Ayizan began to chant aloud, and the group would answer, like in prayer. She sang, in a nasalized, shrill voice, and all joined in. Then the rumbling reverberations of the line of drums resonated in Grace's belly and solar plexus before the vibrations consciously reached her ears. She could hear without seeing the musicians and distinguish minute sounds of the sticks beating on the small hollow drums. The deep thump of the many drums hollowed her sense of perception as the musicians worked the taut skins for a rhythmic melody. And when the short metal clings of the local triangles traveled through the distance, the tingle yanked on a cord located deep within her being.

Grace watched a tall woman by her side and tried to mimic her gestures. She was taller than Grace, at least 5' 10", and she had a pleasant, friendly face. Her skin was light chocolate and only her intelligent eyes could shine brighter than her warm and friendly smile. Dressed in white, she wore two crisscrossed necklaces hanging around her neck and off the opposite shoulder to form an x over her chest. The white scarf in her hand was for Grace, and when she was sure that she wouldn't frighten the girl, with motherly tenderness, she showed how Grace was to wrap it around her head. Now Grace looked like part of the group, everyone had a white scarf. The singsong prayer carried on and then began the dancing. Slowly at first, more participants gathered, and the celebration became livelier. Grace kept the beat but was busy watching Ayizan and not very interested in dancing. The gatekeeper was delicately shredding the fibrous material from palm leaves in her hands and making thinner pieces. This continued until she had a bunch that she tied with a strip. From a string, she made a loop, then a cross and joined them. She tucked the small ankh inside her blouse, close to her heart. Finally, Ayizan took the palm string bunch under her arm and walked strait toward Grace. She didn't have a cane, but looked like she could use one. Grace didn't understand how the vibrant lady had turned into such a vulnerable looking old-bag.

"Bravo Rozalen," she said to Grace's neighbor, "about time someone tied this child's head tied with a white scarf." Grace and Rozalen smiled at each other. Grace quietly memorized the woman's name. Ayizan looked her straight into her eyes.

"Take this, my child and bring it to the next gate. The twins will open the gate, and when they do, give them this bunch of palm leaves and they will gladly let you in."

Removing the small folded shred from its hiding place, Ayizan gave it to Grace.

"Keep this, it has been blessed for you during this ceremony, it is yours." Grace took the palm ankh and tucked it exactly like Ayizan.

Rozalen had moved away when Ayizan began speaking with Grace. She returned to them with full hands.

"Here's for you," she said with a quick smile, "you must be thirsty." She handed Grace a metal cup painted white and filled with water. Grace reciprocated with a smile and drank from the cup, happy to quench her thirst. Rozalen then handed her a square piece of vanilla cake with white icing.

"Here is for energy, you should be ok until you get to gate two, there you will find plenty to eat."

"Thanks," responded Grace right before eating up the cake hungrily; it was pretty good, though a bit hard and heavy, like it had been made at a cheap bakery.

The ceremony was splitting up; most people had had something to eat and drink and were departing. Grace, once again, was hesitant to leave her new friends. Rozalen had stayed close by, attentive to her needs. When it came time for her to go, she encouraged Grace to do the same.

"You should really go now. There is no need for you to be afraid; rid your heart of fear and your mind of useless thoughts and you will not be distracted. Ayizan has purified you; no harm can nor will come of you here in our world-nations. Be on your way with a clear mind and a confident heart; a great adventure lays ahead, trust your destiny." With those words, she kissed Grace on both cheeks, said good bye, and was careful to add that they would meet again soon.

6

THE WAY THE BALL BOUNCED

"Avoidance is better than asking for forgiveness."

We had just won our third game in a row and it was getting harder to see the ball. To my left, the crimson-orange sun seemed like a fireball disappearing into the sea, looking as if it were going for an afternoon swim. Most of the volleyball players   were by now wading in the water, chatting and reliving the high moments of the game. Although the water felt blissfully cool on my skin, and I loved the salty sting in my eyes, I was somehow uneasy being in the ocean at this time. I like to see my toes in the clear water and couldn't now because it was too dark. The little fish that came nibbling at my legs and toes did nothing to ease my discomfort.

It was time to head to the house anyway and find out what had happened to my friends. So I walked out of the water to the spot where I had left my tee shirt and shorts, the sandy carpet were perfect and massaged my feet and toes. Joel joined me quickly; he was more than just uncomfortable, seeming rather jumpy even.

"Canella, wait," he shouted as he joined me on the beach.

"Why are you leaving so quickly? Where are you going in such a hurry?"

I looked at my friend with an uneasy smile, Joel's build and proportions were close to perfect. Call me crazy; to me, he looked like a cross between Tarzan and Jesus—like the former because of his muscular build and savagely tanned skin, and the latter because of his heavyset brows like his father of

26

Middle Eastern descent. Certainly, the mystery that lingered in his blue eyes set him apart. Joel's caramel hair completed his "Tarzan/Jesus" look. Wonder boy spoke French, Creole, English, and Arabic fluently and could communicate in several other languages very well. A well-accomplished martial artist, he also played volleyball and was a pretty decent tennis player. The only reason he wasn't always at the top of his class was that he was constantly inventing, building, and creating stuff that had nothing to do with the strict school curriculum, and that meant time spent away from the books.

"I'm going to the Boulay's, man. I haven't seen Grace since the rarah and I'm starting to worry."

Looking perplexed, he asked:

"What rarah, what happened? What are you talking about?"

So, I told him the story about us in the rarah and the guy who sprayed liquid in my face and how I lost the group; I skipped the part about the wòch sispann but told him that Majis had given me a ride and promised to tell the Boulay family I was at the beach. Joel tried to reassure me.

"I'm sure everything is alright and you will find your friends at home. Let me walk with you, maybe we will run into Toussaint and clear up your worries immediately."

"Are you guys coming to the camp fire later?" he asked

I felt reassured by Joel's comments. Of course, it's all good, and my thoughts quickly moved on to the campfire later that evening.

I imagined a beach party under a full moon, campfires glowing, playing light with the dark; water, fire, earth and wind, the four elements alert to transform the impossible. People would be everywhere, sitting and standing around the fires, singing, dancing, the inspired reciting poetry, and the adventurous making out in the shadows. Sure, I wanted to come to the campfires, so that made me want to hurry home to come back later on.

"Come on Jo, lets walk and we can talk on the way," I suggested leading the way.

"When did you get here?" I asked as we walked toward the thicket of coconut trees bunched on the sides of the road to the house.

"Hatuey and I got here early this afternoon; we caught a ride with Bob."

"Where is Hatuey, by the way, I haven't seen him at all," I said. But Joel hadn't seen him either.

"I guess I'll run into him sooner or later," he said casually. We walked in unison, as if we were marching with a band, but it was coincidental; neither of us tried on purpose to step together, it just happened naturally. Of course we talked more about the afternoon volleyball game and commented on the upcoming championship. By this time we had reached the entrance to Baron's house, where I was staying.

"I'm not going in," he smiled. "I hope to see you later when everything is resolved for the best."

"Thanks a lot Joel, I appreciate the company. I sure hope Grace and I can come to the beach tonight; if not, I'll be out for a swim and ready to play volleyball early tomorrow. See you."

He took my hand into his and captured my eyes in the ocean of his stare, but only for a minute before his funny smile made its move.

"I hope to see you later, Canela." I was stunned and wondered what he was up to. I had known Joel for some time now and he had never shown an interest in me. He was a great guy and good looking and all, but I hadn't considered the possibility of an interest in him. His invitation for that night and his attitude in the water troubled me. I walked onto the small gallery and entered the double doors of the house.

Pisket walked through the door as I came in. "Hi Pisket, what's up?"

"There you are," she said, crooking her neck, eyes wide open. "My mom's been asking about Grace and you for a while now; you 'd better get your slates cleared with the head honcho in the kitchen, if you know what's good for you." I quickly evaluated the meaning of that comment . . . She assumed Grace was with me and Ms. Boulay did too. Hmmm! I asked Pisket:

"How about your dad, do you know if Majis gave him my message?"

Pisket placed her fists on her hips and cocked her head back. "All he could do was drag his ass to bed after dancing until he dropped."

Her tone was fresh, but she had enough sense to whisper her comment. Ok, I needed to think quickly. Was I going into the kitchen to tell Mrs. Boulay that Grace was not with me? If so, I might lose a good opportunity to keep my big mouth shut, getting both of us into more trouble in the process. I thought about this and realized that I couldn't mention that I hadn't seen Grace all day. I decided to look for my friend instead. Didn't Joel say Hatuey was also missing? Maybe the two just happened to be missing together? My best bet was to follow that hunch. I quickly dismissed Pisket:

"Wow, well let me go get Grace and we can talk to your mom, together," and I was out that door in a flash.

It was almost dark outside except for streaks of pinks and purples across the sky. Where was I to begin to look for those two? Where do you look for a couple of teenagers in love? Maybe they were by the beach, under a rock. Perhaps someone had seen them and could tell me more. I started jogging towards the beach to see what information I could gather.

I had to act fast; Pisket would soon tell Mrs. Boulay that I had come home and gone back out to find her daughter, and they would be expecting us soon after that.

A few, early campfires threw some dim light upon the sand itself, but it was hard to recognize people with the dancing flames distorting their faces. I walked near the edge of the water where it licked the sand back and forth. Looking toward the beach occasionally and guessing at silhouettes, I hoped that someone would spot me, walking alone. When I reached the end of the sandy path and rocks obstructed my passage, I turned back and started walking further away from the water this time. I was closer to the people on the beach, but I hadn't yet made out a friendly face. Then Joel came into view, and I saw his gang around a campfire along with other people I didn't really know.

There was a small group of guys seated on metal chairs, strumming guitars, surrounded by a group of young men and women, some seated, most standing. How could I have missed them the first time I walked by? I recognized familiar faces of a few players who trained with the national volleyball team. Joel took my hand:

"Come, let's join the fun." The offer definitely tempted me, but I couldn't loose sight of my purpose here.

"Listen Joel, have you seen Hatuey? I came back out here because Grace wasn't home … I need to find her, the quicker the better."

Joel hadn't seen his friend but was not worried. They didn't keep tabs on each other.

"We deal with each other differently," Joel explained, "When he shows up, it's ok, if he doesn't, that's ok too!"

That won't work for Mrs. Boulay, I thought.

"Well, I guess I just have to keep looking for Grace, with or without Hatuey, then. Sorry, I cannot stay; I will keep looking until I find my girlfriend." I could tell he was not sure what to do, so I smiled and started motioning away.

"See you." He reacted with a jolt, like he had been suddenly been awakened from a dream. "But if you want to go look for Grace, I could come with you. You need a man it is dark outside and there are all kinds of dangers lurking around at night."

Joel took my hand in his and started working on a strategy right away.

"OK, so let's think about this logically," he said. "Where did you last see Grace? Whenever I loose something my mom tells me to back track and repeat what I was doing when I last had the object; let's try doing that for Grace."

Well, I have to admit that I was happy not to be in this alone; his strategy seemed as good as any, and I had no other ideas, so I provided the information.

"I was in the rarah, further than the old hotel, when I first lost sight of her."

Joel decided that's where we would start; it seemed a reasonable option, so we left the beach area and walked towards the road to retrace the steps I had traveled earlier. I brought my hand to my neck and touched the small seed I hadn't thought about since that afternoon. If we were going back, we would have to pass the woch sispann . . . Should I tell Joel what I knew about the seemingly harmless rock? Incredulous myself, I decided not to worry my friend, and pushed the concern to the back of my mind, almost thinking I could make it disappear.

7

THE TWINS ARE AT THE CROSSROAD

"We each have an earring forgotten at the jewelers."

The bunch of palm strips under her arm, Grace was on her way. She had no idea where she was going or how she would get there. Her new friend had told her to free her mind and heart of fear and that's what she was trying to do. She was repeating to herself: trust yourself, trust your destiny, but couldn't help feeling apprehensive about what lay ahead. She didn't even want to think about the possibility she wouldn't find her way out of this parallel world. Somehow, she knew in her gut that the hard part wouldn't be in leaving, but in hanging tough until she found an exit. She set her mind free by remembering everything that had happened to her, trying to make sense of this unnerving and incredible adventure.

Like a movie, the images of the events ran before her mind's eye and she let them come randomly. She reasoned that her mistake had been losing control. She remembered the look in Hatuey's eyes, so warm and inviting; she had completely let down her guard . . . Grace revisited the moment and the feeling of surrendering to him. No resistance whatsoever, he prodded her forward and she was gone! Well, that was a big mistake, she told herself, equating that feeling with her slipping into this other world-nation. She thought about the water and speculated that it would have been a good idea to stay away from the ocean; she promised herself not to forget. She had forgotten about her Jell-O® like surroundings while she sorted these ideas in her head. Then, suddenly, the scene ahead commanded her attention.

Sitting on a great, big yellow and orange swordfish was a man blowing a horn. He was rather heavy set, almost 'balloonish.' Grace realized that many people here shared this characteristic. She noticed the hair, first, as his most distinctive feature. Whoever this person was, he had the funniest hair, long, curly and fuzzy, strands sticking out from everywhere. Seated on the fish, he faced a multicolored hill; in his left hand was a shiny horn that he blew furiously. Even the fish seemed to be making noise, its mouth closing and opening while its long body shook vigorously.

Grace moved closer, noticing that the hill looked like plants and coral but in a variety of shapes and color. All kinds of balls and spikes protruded from it, made of spongy and rugged looking materials; some were still, yet others seemed alive and would move, bob, or sway. Grace moved closer and the man turned and talked to her:

"So you finally got here, can't say you didn't take your sweet time!" Grace turned her head to make sure there was no one behind her; she doubted that the man had intended his words for her.

"You could at least have the common courtesy to excuse your tardiness, or is that too much to ask?" He was looking straight at Grace, apparently addressing her now, for no one else was around. Grace realized he had to be talking to her.

"Excuse me?" She was about to ask why he thought she was late, but Mr. Furious mistook her question for an apology and was happy enough to accept her apology.

"Ok, ok, you're excused; maybe we can get the gate to open now that you are here."

"What gate are you talking about?" Grace sputtered.

"Well," he snapped, pointing with his palm open and extended toward the hill straight ahead of him.

"I'm waiting for THIS gate to open, isn't that obvious?"

Although his tone was blistering, the man looked like a cartoon. He had the sweetest face, with high set cheeks, small squinty eyes that laughed even when he appeared upset. Grace turned toward the hill in time to realize that it indeed was opening. This prompted the man to turn the fish around and ride closer to her:

"Jump aboard my dear, we're going to take you to Legba nation. You will see him at the party tonight; first you meet with the twins, they'll get you settled in."

Grace looked at the friendly-looking man, who added,

"My name is Anthony, by the way. What is yours?" She grew defensive, answering aggressively:

"How is it you were waiting on me but don't know my name?"

"This isn't a blind date, my dear, chill your grill. I'm just doing my friend Rozalen a favor by giving you a ride into Legba nation; if you don't want the ride fine with me."

Grace thought quickly; trust your destiny, Ayizan had said. So she decided to trust that Anthony was part of her destiny and motioned him to come closer so she could climb on behind him.

"They call me Grace, Grace Boulay."

The fish was wide and offered a comfortable passenger seat; she arranged her package between herself and Anthony and laid one hand upon it to hold it securely. They rapidly maneuvered through the gate and into the new world-nation. Grace almost gasped looking ahead; to avoid making any noise she stopped breathing altogether. The big fish glided through the opening and then, swiftly floating, parted the water. The blue sky looked familiar; soft, fluffy clouds and grassy green and brown mounds and hills that almost made her think she had made it home. She let go of the air in her lungs exhaling tentatively. She did not want to believe her senses. They were treading and entering an area with vegetation, but somehow different from what she knew. The land mass was predominantly round; placed here and there were mushroom-like islands sitting on the water. The two-toned islands were sometimes missing a part, the round cakes missing a slice. The symmetry of the plant life was remarkable; cut pizza-style, some mounds had four or more wedges, the colors alternating orange, green, orange, green. The purple and green slices made her wonder whether she had moved on to another level, or whether she was back to reality. Funny what reality can be . . . It means different things to different people, and changes depending upon place. Reality for Grace right now was dealing with Legba-nation and making it through until she could get back to where she was before, with her family and friends.

The fish closed the distance, moving toward a blue and green island. Grace could now see tiny white flowers set against the shiny texture of the blue bushes. Neighboring the blue, bright red tulips shot out from a slice of green grass. The fish went around the island and Anthony turned his head,

"We are getting close," he advised her. When he smiled his jaw shifted involuntarily.

"Listen, I know my way around here, let me talk first. After you meet the twins give them the bundle of palm strings."

"OK." Grace shook her head up and down; whatever, she thought deep down in her heart.

A small group of people, ten or so in number, was standing on the dock. Grace kept her mouth shut as they dismounted the big fish. Anthony, always the perfect gentleman, offered her his hand as she hopped off with the package under her arm. He walked towards the group ahead of her and she shuffled her feet purposely. This allowed her to observe the group while the attention was not yet upon her. She immediately spotted the twins, who reassembled each other like two water drops. She couldn't quite tell if they were boys or girls. They were of normal height, slender, with light skin and short-curly brown hair. The group hovered around an old man she assumed was Legba. Anthony walked straight toward the twins and began chatting quietly with them.

Grace knew he had already mentioned her because all eyes rose to meet hers, which so intimidated her that she quickly lowered her gaze. When Anthony called, she moved carefully towards him and this was good; her behavior showed respect.

"My friends I would like to present Grace, Grace Boulay. She is a friend of Rozalen and Ayizan who prepared this bunch of palm strings and asked her to deliver them to you." Grace sought to make eye contact with a twin, either one, to hand over the package. One of them inched forward to meet her and she handed the bundle over with a shy smile.

"Let me take this, thank you, it will be put to good use." Anthony spoke directly to the twin with the package.

"Naftaly, would you guys mind taking care of Grace and giving her a place to stay? After tonight's festivities, I will be on my way. . . . Anyway, a single man is no proper company for a solitary young lady."

The twins answered together, finishing each other's sentence.

"It'll be great," buzzed one,

"To have company today," piped the other.

The older man and his flock had slowly migrated away from Anthony, Grace and the twins; Grace, in a way, was disappointed not to have met him; she was impatient to practice the greeting Ayizan had taught her.

Anthony took leave of the twins and Grace, promising to see them later and they parted ways.

"My name is Stefany," warbled one twin to Grace.

"My name is Nataly," chirped the other.

"Most people can't distinguish us so they call us both Naftaly for short." They both laughed happily at that comment. Cute, real cute, Grace thought. They continued to walk and the twins cheerfully made conversation.

"So where are you from?" they asked. Grace wasn't sure how to answer the question.

"I live on Earth, and on a small island in the Caribbean ocean," she breathed. "Aha," exclaimed a Naftaly.

"Successor to the Taino civilization."

Grace had studied in school that the Taino Indians existed before the arrival of Christopher Columbus and the Europeans; she learned their disappearance was due to mistreatment and abuse, and they died from the diseases the colonizers had carried to the island. She looked at her deep dark-brown hands and ran her long fingers over her short, coarse and tight-curled hair, taking time to play with the springy little peppercorn balls on the nape of her neck.

"According to my parents, my ancestors came from Africa, but that was a long time ago. I left my friends and family in Port Salut and I hope to go back to them soon." Grace said, saddened by the thought for her family; she really missed them.

Like many twins, the Naftalys were telepathic and could read each other's thoughts. They exchanged one look,

"Well," squawked one twin,

"We wish to help you," finished the other. Grace felt uncomfortable around these two; the way they finished each other's thoughts was aggravating. Just following a conversation was giving her a rubberneck. The frustrating thing though was that she had no choice. At least they seemed inclined to help.

"Thanks for the offer, how can you help me?"

"If you want . . . "

"We can help you find out exactly who your ancestors were." They continued, rapid-fire.

"Also, how to get back home . . . " offered the one twin,

"Will become much clearer after tonight's illumination ceremony," finished the other. The second part of the sentence got Grace's attention; the first part would come back with time. Both Naftalys said in unison,

"Do you know why your name is Grace?" Both stared at her, curious of her response.

8

WHAT YOU SEE IS NOT WHAT YOU GET

"Evil spirits don't scare each other, they eat each other."

Joel and I walked casually along the path that led away from the beach. Increasing our distance from the beach, our walk led us down a more and more empty road. It was completely dark, and the deserted area felt creepy in the dark, probably for both of us. Darkness in these parts implied no electricity, which meant no streetlights either. Instead of sharing worries, we tried to make the conversation lively, taking solace in the comforting noise of our voices.

Volleyball was our common denominator. We talked about our teams and the possibility that we could both soon be playing on the national team. That represented, of course, an exciting possibility. But like a rose with thorns, for those of us in this country it was also an opportunity mixed with many difficulties. A national team carried national expectations, and most people weren't aware of the awful conditions endured by the players.

Then the topic of school came up, another subject with lots of information to share. I really hated mine, a private, Catholic all-girls school, both primary and secondary: St Joseph. Joel's school was mixed, guys and girls, and was a secondary private (but not religious) school. I wished I could go to his school; but I would have to be really good in math but was not – actually, I was a poor student all around. Joel was a relatively good student; that is, his grades were decent B average, and everyone knew he was much smarter and could do better.

"Why do you do so poorly in school, Canela? You're a bright girl; I don't get it."

I didn't get it myself; no matter how much I tried, I was unable to get good grades. I participated in class and sounded smart. I guess I didn't know how to study, or I didn't study enough to memorize the information like my classmates. I read the lessons and made sure I understood them, but that wasn't enough to get good grades.

"Maybe I'm not as smart as you think!" I threw back at him.

As we neared the hotel area, I was hoping to spot Hatuey's car in the lot, and that I might 'discover' him and Grace cuddled up inside. Then, we could pretend we were surprised. We would be sworn to secrecy and all go home and live happily every after. That's exactly how I was hoping to see things happen.

Unfortunately, the parking lot was empty, no cars, nothing. So we kept on walking, according to our agreed-upon strategy, closer to where I had lost the group earlier. Now I knew the wosh sispann was straight ahead; ok, and I was getting worried. I didn't really believe in the stories Majis told, but I didn't think it necessary to test them either. How could I tell Joel it was a bad idea to keep walking forward because of a rock? How could I tell him that going back to the point where I had lost Grace was not such a good idea, either, because earlier on I had a close encounter of the weirdest kind? I was in a fix. Well, I had already told him I might not be as smart as he thought I was; he would now have proof! With every step I took closer to the rock I grew more emotional. My thoughts resounded so loudly in my head I couldn't even hear Joel talking. I turned my attention and focused on his words.

". . . See I've done some reading to prepare a project," his voice trailed, "and it really fascinated me to find out that what you look like is deceptive and doesn't reveal what is present in your DNA."

What was he talking about? I was lost and didn't really care to understand. Hello . . . Anybody home? We were approaching the "Twilight-Zone" a place where evil spirits energized rocks. Shit, how was I going to put this? I couldn't take the time to figure out what he was saying; I needed to stop our quick walk toward disaster. But Joel just kept on talking and talking,

"For example, some dark skin people like the Boulays can have close to fifty percent or more of another race present in their DNA. Get it? They look 100 percent from one race, but are far from being the "pureblood" when it comes down to genetic makeup. Genetics is going to change mentalities about race like nothing before."

The wosh sispann was no longer very far away and this man was oblivious to my despair. I had to invent an escape and it came to me naturally. I tripped and, making more out of it, (my dad always said there was an actress in me)

I fell dramatically, rolled and pretended terrible pain in my ankle. I feigned immobility as I leaned over my bent knee moaning.

"Are you ok? Did you hurt yourself?" inquired Joel absent-mindedly.

I made the fake pain apparent on my face . . . "I'm afraid it's my ankle."

"Well, can you move it?" he asked, now tenderly.

Moving it tentatively at first, I put on a brave face.

"I don't think it's broken," I said making faces. I couldn't really see the expression of his face and he probably couldn't see mine; it was dark and the moon offered little light in the sky.

They say noises carry further and you hear more in the dark because the absence of one sense heightens the awareness of the others. Maybe that's why the clinking metal sound may have seemed far away at first. My ear had picked up the peculiar noise and I was terrorized to imagine what it could be. The distant noise grew closer and I could definitely hear clanging chains; they seemed to be closing in on us quickly. I scrambled to get up, forgetting my ploy,

"Joel, we need to get out of here and fast." I had taken his hand and was pulling him back along our route from the beach. And, of course, he was looking at me like I was crazy.

"Joel, come quick, please; I hear chains, something really creepy is coming this way. Please let's go back to the beach."

"Chains? I don't hear any chains." He balked, cocked his head, and put a hand to his ear to listen more carefully.

"I hear the sound of a percussion instrument like the triangles they play in a rarah. . . . This is probably your rarah coming back, Canela." With a suddenly curious expression he snorted,

"Your ankle was magically healed?"

I was never a good liar, so I decided to come clean.

"My ankle is going to be fine, but I am afraid to go any further because I know there's danger ahead."

"What do you mean, 'danger?' What do you know now that you didn't when you agreed to look for your friend this way?" The clanging sounded closer and closer; I could almost feel the metal against metal dragging in the dirt. It lifted the hairs of my neck and gave me goose bumps. I couldn't hear any other music or beat though, just the sinister cling-cling-clinging noise made by chains dragged over dirt. I pleaded,

"Joel, if this metal noise is from a rarah why is there no beat? No drums? I came through here earlier, okay? I was also here last year, right? I have heard stories. Sure, people do tell all kinds of stories. And I never really paid any attention to them or believed the stories. But now I do!"

"What are you talking about?" Joel finally heard the urgency in my voice and was noticeably nervous.

"Majis told me not to go into this area at night. He mentioned this to me last year; then, this afternoon when he gave me a ride, he reminded me again."

"Ah!" Joel sucked on his teeth and puckered his lips, making what our parents call a rude noise and which Caribbean people make in disgust or exasperation.

"Stories to scare little girls are what Majis told you." At that point, he turned around and marched onward, quickly and undeterred.

"Joel," I shouted, not wanting to move ahead; but I was much too scared to go back alone.

"JOEL!" I screamed, but he kept walking angrily. I had to follow him, willing my resistant body to move forward. I hadn't yet taken ten steps when someone jumped between us. Joel didn't turn around; he just kept walking. The small person didn't face me, obviously concerned with Joel.

"Where the hell do you think you're going?" He shrieked more than shouted, the chain hanging around his shoulders and dangling from his left hand. Joel was standing right next to the cotton-silk tree.

"Yo, Vanilla Boy, that's my tree! Now are you're going to tell me who said you were allowed to stand next to my tree?" The comment stopped Joel in his tracks.

A trained martial artist, Joel turned, head first and body last. In the dark, he had problems making out his challenger, but he immediately sized him up.

"This is public property, peewee, everybody's street. What's up with the attitude, Minnie Mouse? Had a fight with a shrimp this morning and his little claw scratched your neck?" With one swift move, the pygmy creature took the chain from around his neck and threw it around Joel, binding him from the neck down and rendering his arms and legs motionless.

"So what you gotta say now, cat eyes, now you can talk but can't control your body? Beware, banana head, pretty soon I will be controlling your straw-brain thoughts; what are you anyway an overgrown Yellow-bellied Sapsucker?"

Joel wasn't going to back down. "I really hate that . . . a pipsqueak with a big mouth." Joel answered calmly as though he didn't notice the chains snaked around his body.

I had not moved from my spot; I tried not to breathe, hoping and praying the brownie didn't turn around and take notice of me. After capturing Joel in the chains he had moved closer to his prey and had put more distance between us; the more the better was my opinion. I knew that I had to release Joel and hoped the magic words would do just that, but I didn't know when to say the sentence Majis had taught me. The dwarf tugged on the chains and for the first time Joel reacted with a twitch of his body. The midget started sniffing around my friend,

"Mmmm, imported swine, pink and prime, a rare treat for me indeed."

"*Tantin, tonton, tantin tann tonton,*" I started to chant. "*Tantin, tonton, tantin tann tonton,*" I chanted louder;

"*Tantin, tonton, tantin tann tonton!*" The chains loosened from around my friend and fell to his feet. The dwarf turned to me in rage,

"Who the hell are you?" he hollered. Joel was swift and moved quickly, while the dwarf took short hopping steps. He had caught up to the dwarf by the time the small man was by my side.

"Now there are two of us and half of you." Joel boasted. "I don't fight unfair situations, why don't you beat it you little runt?"

The gnome began to growl and was about to pounce on both of us when the headlights of a car disturbed the mystery of the night. The vehicle was following the path toward us. I watched the gremlin hobble frantically back to the property he guarded. Intrigued, I continued to watch him as he suddenly stopped and brought a shiny straw to his lips. What could he be doing? I wondered. After Joel suddenly brought his hand to his thigh, the idea that it might be a dart gun entered my mind; the possibility of a poisoned dart was not far behind. With a wicked scowl on his face, the brownie looked back in our direction and disappeared. Holding his leg Joel took my hand and we moved to the side of the road as the car came to a stop. It was the Boulay's Citroen.

Mr. Boulay's, head perched out of the driver's window, turned to me.

"Young lady, what are you doing alone in the dark in the company of this young man? Get in the car immediately!" I froze, but Joel didn't loose his cool.

"With your permission, sir, I would like to say that we are not together. I'm just accompanying Canela for her safety as she searches for her lost friend."

Dad Boulay looked at me then at Joel and mumbled through his teeth:

"Get in the car, both of you, NOW!" We scrambled over, Joel dragging his leg as we both jumped into the back seat.

9

FAITH SAVES

"Not all illness can be cured by a doctor."

"My dear, Grace implies life with the Father through the gift of the spirit. The spirit heals and sanctifies our souls, and enables us to participate in eternal life. Your name is Grace and you have a gift, an unmerited favor through God's intervention, his gratuitous initiative." The Naftalys seemed very self-assured. "You're here to find out about yourself and your life path."

Grace wondered how she could ever have thought this place looked like home. On second thought, it looked more like a pastry float in a parade. Nature here seemed measured, calculated and tamed . . . measured out like the ingredients that go into a recipe. Vegetation cut to precision, rounds and curves, not a leaf out of place. The island mounds around her formed colorful slices, an appetizing sight for the eyes. The houses they passed were few and far in between. Grace wondered how far they had to go.

"So, do we still have to walk very far?"

"Just a short way to go," replied one Naftaly,

"Only a bit further ahead," continued the other.

"Explain to me about the gift; I don't understand. Will I be getting a gift at the party tonight?" Grace asked and they continued to walk. The Naftalys looked at each other, rolling their eyes in unison and shaking their heads in disbelief.

"No, you won't get a gift during tonight's celebration. It's not a birthday party; it's an illumination ceremony to see more clearly where you must go and what you will have to do." The Naftalys sounded impatient that Grace didn't seem to understand the evening's events.

Grace snapped back. "Fine, I'm not stupid, okay; I just don't know the system in your world here. So what's the story with the gift, where does it fit into my name?" The other twin took the cue and started explaining again.

"It's the name Grace, in itself, that implies the gift or unmerited favor."

Naftaly approached a white metal gate and pushed it open. They were in front of a small, pink, cinder-block, two-story house. The front garden smelled of mint and citronella. In the background, the melody of tiny insects played in the night. Square glass windows fit into a checkerboard pattern of blue, yellow, and green cement blocks.

Through the front door they walked into a large room with no separations. A wooden statue of a Maroon blowing a conch shell and carrying a book in his left hand stood in a rectangular opening of the only wall. To the right of the wall, glass doors led to a stone-paved terrace. Stefany took the package of palm strings towards the kitchen on the left while Nataly led Grace to the couch next to the glass doors.

"This couch opens into a bed; this is where you will be sleeping tonight. Our room is upstairs; it's just one big bedroom and we each have a bed. This is our extra bed." The twin gestured for Grace to sit, so she perched herself on a corner of the couch, feeling out of place.

"If you wish to take a shower, please do." Naftaly winked at her twin. "I'm sure we could come up with something appropriate for you to wear tonight."

At first, Grace had felt uncomfortable wearing the long blue skirt the twins had offered. She usually wore jeans, except for her school uniform, a skirt and jumper, which was one of the reasons she didn't like skirts. However, when she looked around at the gathering and noticed that all women and girls were wearing skirts, she was happy to blend in with the crowd.

Twenty people were already there when they arrived. The lives in the houses and huts of this small village revolved around their ruler Legba and his teachings. He was the second gatekeeper because he could open the way. The people who would participate in the night's ceremony were his people. Like everywhere, some were good, some bad, each in a special way. The Naftalys went around and presented Grace to friends and acquaintances.

She had noticed Anthony seated under a tree, tugging on his ratty beard and listening intently to a group of young men in conversation. The Naftalys escorted Grace one on each side; she was still unable to tell them apart. The men talked about the traditions kept in Legba nation since the beginning, proud that they had not been altered in any way.

"You will participate in most of the celebration; yet some rituals are only for the initiates' eyes, so you will not be allowed. First come the prayers, then the lighting of the candles and the dance. Meanwhile, the offerings will be set out and finally the party will be open to everybody. "

The Naftalys offered bits and pieces of information as they headed toward the biggest structure in the compound. The three casually climbed up the steps and entered a big circular room. Grace was surprised to see that she had to go back down a few steps once inside. Three big inside steps for sitting ringed the room, as with an arena; the built-in seats all offered a great view of the center, where the dance was to occur.

The inside of the building reminded Grace of a beehive because of the round shape and the many doors and openings leading to hallways that opened onto more rooms. Grace would soon learn about the network of people and the rituals they performed by participating in the Legba nation belief system.

"Not a lot of people here. We're here to go inside," blurted a Naftaly.

"We will be joining the prayers," said the other. They went toward the left side of the room and exited through the first side door. That door led through a semi-dark hallway. Grace noted a glow of light at the end of the narrow hall; the cement-grey ceilings hung low and put her nerves on edge. Increasing feelings of apprehension and fear grew within her. She wondered what in fact would happen here. She could hear singing coming from the room; a feminine voice leading and others joining in the chorus. They reached the doorway and entered the room from the back; Grace hoped their arrival would remain unnoticed.

Women dressed in white, with white scarves tied around their heads, filled half of the room. She carefully listened to the prayer they were reciting:

All in the presence of the Lord
And the angel of God said to Mary
Come Lord come
O Jesus, come to me through the Eucharist
Holy Virgin sanctify us
Lord, I believe your presence in the Host
Alas, alas Madeleine
Sente zan-y, sente san-y
Hail Mary
Grace Mary grace
Saint Philomena virgin martyr
Grace Mary grace
You who live with pain

Grace Mary grace
Saint Francis begs the faithful to pray.

The prayer ended. Naftaly prodded Grace with her elbow and they made their way to the front of the group. The prayer leader had a big steel cup that she handed to Grace; it was full of water and was somewhat heavy in her left hand. She tried to shift the cup to her right hand, but Naftaly nudged her again; the twin shook her head to indicate the negative, instead she lit a candle that she thrust into Grace's right hand.

A small group of women led Grace into a back room where a pipe hung from a rusty nail under an archway. On a nearby table sat the picture of Saint Peter, a set of keys, a few packs of cigarettes, and several small mirrors. A walking stick and a pair of crutches dangled from the room's ceiling.

"Face north," Naftaly instructed Grace, pointing her in the right direction.

"With a controlled gesture, move the cup forward and make a small quantity of water fall to the floor." Grace executed the gesture and furtively looked into the twin's eyes to see if she had done it correctly; Naftaly's head nodded in approval. Next the twin turned Grace around 180 degrees to the right. Now facing south, Grace was instructed to repeat the water offering gesture. Grace was asked to rotate to her right a quarter turn, 90 degrees, and to make another water offering. Another 180 degree turn and Grade was facing east, where she made a final water offering. She made one final quarter turn to the right, and arrived back at the starting point.

Naftaly took the candle. The big metal cup was only half-full but felt very heavy nonetheless and Grace was happy to be able to hold on to it with both hands. The water offering finished, the group went back to the prayer room to find it empty. Everyone had headed to the main round arena and Grace, the twins and the other members of the smaller group were about to join them.

Grace noticed the main room was now full of people and it disturbed her that so many strangers could be watching her during the ceremony. She was more and more nervous facing this unknown. She looked to the center of the floor. Around a big pole she didn't remember noticing before was old man Legba creating some sort of design on the ground. Her group moved closer to take their places, and she could see that the old man was working on a series of geometrical shapes and interconnected lines. Legba created this design with a cream-colored powder that he would let sift through his fingers. The contrast against the brown dirt revealed the details; circles and diamonds, curvy lines, stars, and letters to create an intricate pattern.

The drums were in a line; straggling musicians took their places sluggishly. Later than sooner, the drums started to rumble. One player would call another with a drumbeat, then others would join in a playful melody of percussions, beats, and rhythms. At last, Legba placed the twenty-one candles on their spots in his intricate design; the drum rhythms went from playful to pertinent. Swaying to the beat, Legba lit the candles one at a time, starting on the left, and finishing on the right. Then voices began to chant. Nasalized, shrieking, rhythmic voices,

 ♪*Open the gate for Atibon, Papa Legba passing by e ♪ e ♪ a ♪ watch your step ♪ Watch your step oh father Legba watch your step. ♪*

Legba looked old and worn, like he carried a heavy load of years. The singers handed him a pipe and a straw bag that he draped over his left shoulder. He puffed on his pipe, looked around in the crowd, and walked straight to Grace. She saw him headed for her and knew this was a decisive moment. Her heart raced. Deafened by the blood pounding against her eardrums and the echo of vibrating drums, she watched Legba walk her way. She was so scared that she froze but somehow managed to recall the greeting Ayizan had taught her well. She anticipated the *papa* lwa's handshake. But Legba made

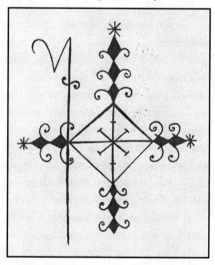

a move that took her off-guard. He hooked his pinkies in hers, and began to twirl. They twirled in short, hurried steps, touching the crowns of their heads; under and over, their hands linked and stretched out in front of their faces, they spun . . . right to left and back again, left to the right.

"Trouble is headed your way," he gasped breathlessly, although he had completed the contortions of the complicated ritual gestures relatively easily for such an old man.

"First you must resolve your past issues, only then you can move on."

This was the message Legba had for her. After saying his piece, he was ready to move on. Looking affectionately into her eyes, he softened,

"Be courageous my child," he advised, before joining the singing and dancing crowd. He had other messages and continued to deliver them to each recipient, working his way around the room in his careful, slow pace.

What past issues? Grace's head started to spin. What had she done to the universe that was so important that this underworld was her punishment? How could she 'resolve' the issue, she didn't even know what it was! Was this about Hatuey? The thought dawned on her again. Her mom had warned her about having a boyfriend; she forbade it until Grace turned eighteen. Okay, so she felt free and uninhibited with him dancing in the rarah; his hands had found her hips and she had let him flatter her firm and shapely body. When he locked his arms around her shoulders she had let herself go to the feeling of warmth and giddy uneasiness, and she would admit that her back had snuggled to find his muscular body. They stuck like magnets; they were dancing in unison effortlessly, as though each anticipated the other's next move. His head behind hers, he had nuzzled the space between her neck and ear, his warm breath tickling her; and she had enjoyed it. The nuns had warned her about the punishment for carnal sins—sins of lust, the nuns at school had called them. She hadn't thought about this in the rarah, but she sure was wondering now . . .

Succumbing to a panic attack, Grace's heart began to race. She thought she was likely to faint; her feet felt dead, her legs weighed her down like cement pillars. Like a horse about be mounted by a rider, she felt the weight of a being sitting on the nape of her neck. This dread visitor made its way into her body, displacing any little self-command she had left. She fell asleep, or fainted, or went in a coma; in other words, her conscious self was switched off. The bizarre part was that her body kept moving.

For those who were around, the change in her was apparent immediately. Stefany and Nataly looked at Grace as her body trembled; she shuddered like she was freezing-cold. Then, her arms jerked to her sides, and her legs acted like soft springs that made her dance up and down, bending her knees. She seemed transformed: her big, round eyes lay in their sockets like eggs over-easy; in place of yolk on white were two fiery red disks. Grace was having difficulty talking, she stuttered, *ta ta ta ta ta, ta ta ta* but acted exuberantly, communicating through ample gestures that immediately attracting a small crowd.

Stefany knew what to do. First, she tied the shiny blue scarf around Grace's head. Nataly drew a medium-sized bottle of cologne from her bag; the familiar long neck bottle wrapped in silver paper foil had a black plastic top. A rectangular white label with red roses and other flowers depicted a young lady from a past century with a bird perched on her left hand: Florida Water, just what *Ezuli* would want. Stefany offered the bottle to the coquettish Ezuli-cum-Grace, who doused herself lavishly. *Ta tat a tat a tat* . . . Ezuli certainly had something to say and was making that clear; what she was saying was much less obvious. The twins knew they had to get Legba, for he was the only one who could understand what she was trying to communicate. They would have wanted to take her to him, but Ezuli-cum-Grace had plans of her own and she certainly wasn't going to wait for the twins to tell her what to do.

With a resolute step, Ezuli-cum-Grade walked strait to the back room where food had been laid out in offering. Without being invited, she helped herself with both hands, stuffing her mouth with fistfuls of the offerings prepared for the lwa. Legba and the twins approached her slowly; he ordered them to giver her a drink of orange soda. Stefany and Nataly knew better than to question Legba's orders. After filling a cup, they literally held her down and poured the soda forcibly through her clenched teeth. Ezuli-cum-Grace her cheeks bulging with the liquid still in her mouth, got up and grabbed a young initiate standing close by. She held the unwilling young girl's head in her hands and proceeded to give her a mouth-to-mouth infusion of the soda. Once set free, the young initiate spit it out, totally disgusted, and attempted to run away; but the possessed Ezuli-cum-Grace was unusually strong and yanked her back. *Tat tata tatatatat tat,* she stuttered menacingly; Legba interpreted what she was saying,

"Tell that up-to-no-good bitch Grace that I'm looking forward to witnessing her lose her precious hymen; I'll laugh my head off when she gives it up willingly . . . Too bad I didn't have that chance: mine was stolen and vilified. She can relax while she's down here, though; she is far away from the dangers of her beloved's seduction. But she's mine for now! And I'll make her life miserable until I am offered my animal sacrifice. I delivered a fortune to her ancestors and they failed to give me the one thing I requested. HOW DARE THEY OFFEND ME! She can kiss her beau, her family, and the world good bye as far as I'm concerned." And Grace crumbled, legs first, folding to the ground like an empty towel.

Stefany and Nataly slid a hand under each armpit and carried her to the closest chair. They sat there a long time while resting and listening to the noise of the ceremony in the next room. When Grace regained consciousness, she was between the two. Like many people after channeling, she remembered nothing. Her thoughts took off where she had left them, thinking about Hatuey. Coincidentally Stefany asked her right then,

"Do you have a boyfriend back home, Grace?" It was too dark to see her blush, but she felt like a child caught with a hand in the cookie jar.

"Why do you ask? She answered defensively. The twin answered amused,

"Let's just say, the information came from your mouth." Grace worried about what she had done, and especially said, during her loss of consciousness.

"What happened to me? What did I do?" The twins tried to calm her worries.

"We're going to give you the facts; you deal with them, fair?" She looked perplexed. She turned right, then left, looking into each twin's eyes imploringly. DAMN! She had no choice.

"Ok, tell me everything, I can handle it."

10

THE NEWS SPREAD LIKE CRUNCHY PEANUT BUTTER

"You must go there to know there."

A thick silence hung over the car, covering its occupants. Dad Boulay was speeding his old Citroen over a patch of bad dirt road and it squeaked and banged with every bump. He seemed really upset, I had a feeling that a sermon was coming and I wouldn't have to wait long.

"Canela, I've known your father all my life. My oldest and fondest memories go back to kindergarten; I have a mental picture of us in shorts playing together, like all the other little boys our age, back in the day. After that, we went to the same primary school and joined the boy scouts together; we were in the same troop: the Castors. We have been more than good friends, brothers, for as long as I can remember, and I don't want that to change. He has trusted me and allowed you to come here with my family because he knew I would treat you like my own daughter and not allow any harm to come to you. He wouldn't forgive me if something were to happen to you because of carelessness . . . I wouldn't forgive myself.

Mr. Boulay was good at making me feel bad, real bad. I felt I had betrayed his trust. When I thought about it, however, I realized that I hadn't done anything wrong; so why was I feeling so bad? Joel jumped into the conversation at the first opportunity.

"Mr. Boulay, I think you should know we were looking for Grace."

A few seconds went by before Jack Boulay registered the news.

"What to do you mean, exactly, when you say you were looking for my daughter Grace; it is my daughter we are talking about, young man?"

Joel responded in a calm voice.

"Yes sir, we were looking for your daughter, Grace. Canela hasn't seen her since the rarah this afternoon and was searching for her. I offered to keep her company and to help her look."

Jack Boulay took some more time to process the new information.

"Canela," he said and exaggerated the calm voice, "break it down for me and tell me step by step when you last saw Grace and what you have done since then."

"Ah well . . . Ok," I hesitated and just blurted out the rest: "Basically, I lost Grace in the rarah this afternoon. I got side-tracked and lost the group; so I went back to the beach and played volleyball with Joel and some other players."

"What happened after the beach volleyball?" demanded Mr. Boulay.

I thought about the way I had snuck in and out of the house that afternoon.

"After the game, Joel walked me home and I met Pisket. She told me Grace wasn't home, so I returned to the beach to find out if anyone had seen her. Instead, I found Joel again, and he agreed to walk with me to the last place I had seen Grace this afternoon, to pick up her trace. We were walking to that place when you found us, end of story, honest Mr. Boulay." Joel winked at me discreetly; I knew I had explained it right.

"We have to find Majis right away; he'll know who to see to get to the bottom of this." Daddy Boulay voiced his thoughts, but his words didn't seem intended for either Joel or me.

Dad Boulay's Citroen lulled over the sandy path to Majis' house where we quickly learned he was out. He was close by, however, so we headed there. Soon enough, the old car approached the clearing where, under a round, straw top, four men were seated, playing dominoes on a square sheet of plywood resting on their knees. Oddly, Majis wasn't among them.

Joel and I sat in the car observing Dad Boulay talk to the men. We hadn't spoken to each other since we got into the car. I tried an old joke to break the ice,

"What's the matter man, cat got your tongue?" and I tried poking his ribs to get a reaction, which didn't work . . . at first. Then came a characteristic Caribbean expression of disgust, (Jamaicans call it "sucking teeth") and he hissed while shaking his head.

"Hell of a mess you got me into, Canela." I was surprised at his tone: he was angry, which threw me off guard. I hadn't asked or even insisted that he accompany me; HE had. Wait a minute here! Why was he angry with me?

"I got you into? Since when did I become responsible for what you decided to do?"

"Let the truth be told," he grunted, "I wouldn't have believed you even if you had told me what was going to happen. Hell, it did happen and I still don't believe it, though I was there! Canela! What in God's name was back there?! Do you know?"

I thought about the strange little gnome, which gave me chills and goose bumps once again. I had been warned many times not to go to certain areas at night because they were dangerous. Even so, I went there knowingly and stared the face of danger in the eyes. This was bound to happen.

"I tried to tell you that I had heard stories; but I hadn't really believed them either. Who could have known that the stories weren't just stories to scare little girls?"

I really hadn't appreciated him mocking me earlier.

"By the way, how's your leg?" He didn't answer and turned his head to look at Mr. Boulay walking back toward the car with Majis. I could tell by the tilt in his head that Majis was trying to identify who was inside the car. His casual walk revealed his easy-going personality.

"Hello, hello everybody," As always, Majis was very friendly, his peppery cologne floated inside the car as he plopped into the front seat.

Dad Boulay started the engine and we were on our way back to Majis' house just around the corner. After stopping the car, Jack Boulay motioned to Joel,

"Come with me young man, we have a pending conversation I would like to take outside." Joel stepped out bravely, though his leg buckled under him. Before anyone could react, he corrected his step.

"You ok?" Majis asked.

"Nah . . . nothing," muttered Joel, who was then on his way, but not before turning slowly in my direction and making eye contact.

Not missing a beat, Majis hammered each word. "Canela I need you to tell me the whole story, step by step, so that I can understand what happened to Grace this afternoon."

Joel had no idea that his conversation with Jack Boulay would turn out the way it did. What he learned that night was to stay with him forever; it formed his judgment and helped him understand the place called the Caribbean over time and through history. In short, Mr. Boulay explained to him that different civilizations had explored the seas and sailed to America way before Columbus was born.

Records of those travels exist from China to Africa, in India and Europe. There are religious documents, written testimonials, and oral traditions that back up this fact. Nowadays archeological discoveries are confirming all of these sources.

When you look for well-known sailing expeditions, the Bible is one of the first and obvious sources for such tales. Many people regardless of their creed have heard about Noah; the story is that he built an ark and traveled around the world with animals selected two by two, after it rained for forty days and forty nights. Noah, the Bible tells us, had three sons: Ham, Shem and Japheth.

Joel had heard about Noah, but nothing of his sons. Since he was expecting a lecture about right and wrong, (now from a biblical perspective) he didn't really pay attention when Jack Boulay mentioned that in the presence of an angel Noah divided the earth among his three sons.

Jack Boulay had lost the young man's attention while relating the Bible story. To get his attention back, he asked him how one proves information to be valid. Joel had no idea what to answer; he really hadn't listened and did not care about what Mr. Boulay was explaining.

"To verify a story, check several sources." And Jack Boulay continued with his story; this time Joel listened more carefully. That's how we see that in European history, specifically Irish beginnings, they pick up the thread of Noah's descendents." Jack Boulay had lost Joel again.

Although somewhat impressed with the history and story-telling skills, Joel had little interest in Bible fables or Irish legends. But the next question Jack would ask him would start a crack in the solid educational foundation that had taught him that Columbus had discovered America.

So then, Boulay told him about Timbuktu and Joel wondered why he said it would be easier to handle. He patiently explained that the city was famous because of its scholars and intellectuals who taught in the prestigious universities there. This civilization had a glorious period long before Columbus removed the cover of several Caribbean islands. Joel tried to concentrate on what the man was saying. Timbuktu was part of a major African Mandingo kingdom the size of Europe and its outstanding reputation was legendary worldwide.

"Now while you're wondering why I'm talking about the Mandingo intellectual capital of Africa, I'm going to ask you to think about the answer to a question." Joel paid close attention, eager to find a way to impress this man. "How could it be that, according to a Harvard linguist named Leo Wiener, the Mandingo language had left linguistic markers in the New World in beginning of the 15th century.

Joel was puzzled. He turned the possibilities in his head. "Linguistic markers" is a fancy way to say "words" that take some time before they are absorbed into a language. That would mean that the Mandingo people would have to have made contact with the natives and some useful words had remained. He also thought that the Mandingo people needed be important both in numbers and probably in status for that to happen. When he thought about it, Joel had reached the conclusion that Mandingo people were probably in the area before Columbus. Wow, he needed to rethink his impossible logic! How about this professor, what are his credentials?

Instead of talking, Joel's mouth turned to cotton. As if the dentists' aspirator had sucked the saliva from his mouth, he was so terribly thirsty and felt nauseous. All of a sudden he started to sweat thick drops that beaded like giant goose bumps all over his forehead; they slipped over his brows and into his eyes and down his nose and gushed down his face and neck. He tried to wipe his face with the back of his hand. When he looked again, the midget was in front of him; he jumped back, shook his head and it was Boulay again. Gradually, a warm wave of drowsiness melted over him.

Mr. Boulay noticed the young man's distress.

"Son, are you ok?" Joel heard Boulay's voice in the distance, but it didn't seem to matter. Instead, he became unaware of his thoughts and tuned into a deeper self. He honed into this inner serenity and the outside world dissipated and then disappeared.

"Joel, are you all right young man!" Mr. Boulay shook his shoulder. Instead of jolting him back to consciousness, the abrupt gesture caused the young man to crumple to the ground softly, almost like a bed sheet. He felt himself fall but could do nothing to control his body. He was seeing too many layers to be able to process all of the images at once. His eyes looked at Mr. Boulay, then at Canela and Majis hovering over him. He could see them and knew his eyes were open; he couldn't change that either. He had no command over any muscle in his body.

On another level, as if through a third eye, he could see the midget. The sinister brownie was standing there, looking and smirking, but he never approached Joel. He remained a threat lurking in the background of his immediate surroundings. The most fascinating part of this episode was the storybook reality happening in the foreground of his brain. This reality was like a movie; although there were vivid images running across his eyes, Joel was detached and could not change anything. He was merely a spectator. Then, he felt his eyes close and was conscious that he couldn't look at the people around him anymore. He remained, nonetheless, quite aware of his surroundings.

Mr. Boulay and Majis weren't sure what to do with Joel. They didn't want to move him, especially because he seemed to have fallen into a peaceful sleep. They decided to leave him with Canela and Majis' wife.

They two men took off in the Citroen, planning to notify Grace's mom about her disappearance and to find a doctor to examine Joel. It was late at night on a holiday weekend, but they were hopeful a friend of Majis' would be home and would agree to help them.

Mr. Boulay asked me to sit next to Joel and not leave his bedside.

"Canela, I want him to see a familiar face when he wakes up." Dad Boulay was always so optimistic. I did what I was told. We were in enough trouble already. I remembered the conversation with Majis earlier. His coal eyes had burned holes through my pretenses, and the answers he wanted had danced out of me like snakes responding to charmers. I had nothing to hide anyway. I knew he wanted to establish Hatuey's involvement in Grace's disappearance, but I was honestly unable to answer those questions, I really had not seen Hatuey. I looked over at Joel and he seemed to be resting peacefully. I had my own theory about what had happened to him and couldn't wait to verify my hypothesis.

I had to be alone with no one watching, which that took some time and patience, but was easy. I waited until Mrs. Majis was busy somewhere far from the room. Once the coast was clear I tiptoed around the bed to look at my friend's legs. He had on shorts and this helped. I tried to find the right thigh he grabbed just before we got into the Boulay's car. Sure enough, there was a red spot and the area was warm and tender; Joel moaned every time I touched it. I was positive that the midget had shot him with a poisoned dart. It must have been very light and had fallen off after breaking skin. I know I had seen the metal straw shine from the evil little man's mouth. OK, I had a poison antidote around my neck since my encounter that afternoon; so, how could I give it to him without arousing suspicion?

All I needed was a cup of hot water.

11

$\mathcal{B}$ACK TO OUR PRESENT

"Chickens shouldn't laugh at turkeys' funerals."

"Naftaly help me figure this out," Grace said to the twin standing to her right.

"I feel like my thinking skills are in slow motion, and I need to understand now." Both twins understood her plight and both were ready to help, hoping she would accept the information they were about to share with her.

"I will be glad to share with you our representation and classification of places, people, and things. I hope this information will help you understand your place and time in your world."

"I look at you and see you in the flesh," continued the other twin, "but you, Grace, are much more. When you look around and see our nation, you see colors, shapes, and texture. But I can assure you this place is much, much more."

"I think you will understand better if I start with your first people and their story. Although I don't yet know your specific family history, I do know that if you are here you belong to the people of the first. With a strand of hair, a nail clipping, or a swab of saliva, geneticists can establish your specific lineage to your clan from the first-people. Humans walked upright in the Old World and from there emigrated, populating other lands on earth. You can follow a direct line however, through the matriarchal nucleic DNA; that is, the DNA from your mom. Your human body carries your personal code or genetic combination. This body in the flesh must face its essence in spirit; we call the life energy *nanm*.

In your case, your basic programming is why you are here, unbeknownst to what you call your conscious self or awareness, which brings us to the next element; we call this duality within all humans the *bonanj*. We think you have two: a major one and a minor one; all-living beings share a life force that connects us all to the universal energy. Your major or outer *bonanj* called *gwobonanj* is that part of the cosmic life force that passes into the newly formed human being; it will keep the body alive and sentient and after death will pass back into the reservoir of energy in the cosmos. The major *bonanj* is like your own team of angels; it is one-half of what Catholics call the soul.

The other half of the soul is the minor or inner *bonanj*: the *tibonanj* represents the accumulation of a person's knowledge and experiences and it is responsible for determining an individual's characteristics, personality, and free will."

Somehow, that perception of the duality of the soul made sense to Grace: both a part of the whole and a separate individual. She often felt that inner tug between what she would want for herself, against the pressures of society, and even her peer group. It was as if an invisible force fought to determine the turn of some events. At times, she had given in to her friends not being able to resist their pressure, not necessarily because she really wanted to go along personally. She thought back to the spirit of the flesh and needed more time to figure this part out; but the other Naftaly left no time for thought.

"We distinguish a final element to complete the description of a human, called the *zetwal,* or star, which, my dear, is destiny that comes knocking, is what the stars have reserved for you during this life time. The *zetwal* is tricky because so much depends on individual will and choices. For us, the star symbol has a special meaning, it represents the five elements present in human beings."

Both Naftalys stopped talking almost on cue; they were home. The conversational pause was convenient. Turning the key through the hole in the yellow door and they were all inside the house.

"Are we calling it a night now, or would you like to continue this conversation, Grace?" By all means, Grace wanted more information.

"Please," she said to her companions, "let's continue; it's really important I get a better handle on things."

"Ok, are you with us so far? Did we express ourselves clearly? Tell us . . . " Here Grace cut them off. Surprisingly, she felt that their classification presented no real problems for her; it made sense. She recited the elements of existence with confidence:

1. body,

2. life energy: *nanm*;

3. the major *bonanj: gwobonanj* ;

4. the minor *bonanj*—like inner and outer consciousness: *tibonanj* ;

5. and destiny: *zetwal.*

6. She was ready to hear more, eager to tie these new facts in with the events that had occurred that evening.

"So what happened to my bonanj tonight? Seems to me some part of it checked out for a while and let some other energy move my body." The Naftalys looked at each other with a smile, noting that she had accepted and integrated the notions in her head.

"Four things happened. The drums you listened to tonight were not casual musical percussions, but crucial elements of ageless rituals. Therefore, first, your body responded to millions of years of programming; the drum vibrations traveled through your neurons and transmitted messages to your central nervous system." Funny, Grace thought to herself. I could never dance as well as most of my friends and now I'm the one with a basic programming that responds to vibrations. Naftaly waited a while to make sure Grace was following and had understood and then continued.

"If you understand that your body reacted because of its innate components, I ask you to step up one level and see that your nanm is intimately attached to your body and was prepped to participate in the occurrence that happened tonight. Before we continue, maybe we should discuss what you don't remember of the evening's events."

The comment made Grace uneasy. She remembered she had blanked out a part of the evening; she had talked about Hatuey. Nevertheless, she didn't know what or how much she had revealed and she didn't like having her business aired in public. Why did the twins want to bring this up again?

"If you guys don't mind, I'd rather not talk about Hatuey; seems like he's the one responsible for my being here, and if I hadn't followed his enticing lead I probably would be home right now. I don't think I'll be following him ever again . . . anywhere."

"One-step forward, three steps back." The twins exchanged the phrase telepathically, realizing that Grace had not really put all the elements together in order to understand her situation yet!

"Ah listen, you may have been with your friend when you crossed into our world-nations; but only you have been called, which probably has nothing to do with your feelings for Hatuey or any one else. You being here, Grace, is all about you. At the illumination ceremony, you proved to be a medium; *Ezili Jewouj* came to life before our eyes through you. She mounted *you* and spoke through your mouth, and it was she who divulged the physical nature of your relationship with Hatuey."

"Ezili, je huh? What are you guys talking about? Mounted? Me, a medium? You've totally lost me"

"Maybe it's getting too late," said Naftaly looking conspicuously at the other twin. "We can pick up this conversation tomorrow with a fresh mind. You're probably very tired, and we are too." Naftaly stifled a yawn. "Maybe we should call it a night."

"NO WAY! A night . . . not now. You're telling me I was mounted in one sentence and good night in the next. I'm sorry, but you must tell me what happened at the ceremony for me to understand!" Grace's head was racing at the speed of light; she was a medium! Why was she a medium? She nearly screamed, "Why do you call me a medium?"

Although exhausted, the Naftalys didn't mind staying up to provide Grace with an explanation. Whether she was open to accept it was another story. They did not control this; only she did. Free will, one of the most precious and challenging gifts humans receive.

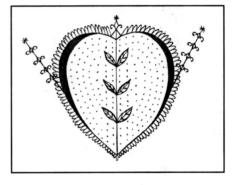

"My dear, this is what I know: mediums are those whose have bonanj that can easily be displaced; they are people with what you might call flexible bonanj. Tonight, we saw your body in front of us, but it was commanded by Ezili. Everyone knew this instantly.

The realization of what the twin was saying pushed Grace into a special moment called an epiphany. She could hear new sounds and modulations. Or was it that she could now see better, like she had a sixth sense? As if she had ripped through the protective veil of her limited vision into another dimension, she felt like she could all of a sudden see the light of truth.

OK. Come to think of it . . . this new information could be cool, Grace thought to herself. She had channeled Ezili energy, wicked! Channeling: she was okay with this; but, possession? This sounded scarier. Then red-hot reality came knocking. What's an Ezili, and what did she say using my mouth?" Grace wondered and immediately asked Naftaly.

"Ezili is a feminine energy with a dual nature: Freda, the coquettish feminine seductress, presents herself as a wealthy white woman. She is perceived as a promiscuous love goddess who moves in an atmosphere of perfume and luxury. Ezili Danto is pictured in the lithographs of Saint

Barbara Africana with tribal scars upon her cheeks. She is a hard worker, and will give you the strength to overcome adversity along with the confidence to stand up for yourself."

"Last night, a Danto guard, Jewouj, speaking through you, said that you needed to fulfill a debt to her before you be released back into your world. She claims your ancestor promised her an animal sacrifice and didn't deliver; it's a bad practice to make promises you don't keep, especially to powerful spirits."

"Wait a minute! How can I be accountable for promises someone I never knew has made! This is crazy!" Grace's patience was wearing thin.

Naftaly answered patiently, "If Ezili says your ancestor made a promise, you better believe she knows exactly who she's talking about. You may not know your relative, but she does. Of all the Ezilis, Jewouj is the most vindictive; her fiery red eyes are the telltale sign of her hot temper. But she is fair and will only ask for what she is due. Who do you think could accomplish this delicate mission for you? It must be someone you trust." Someone she trusted? Grace tried to think about home, but it seemed so far away. How could she transmit a message to people back home?

"Wouldn't it be impossible to contact someone from my home?" A short silence fell over the room. Grace looked at one, then the other twin . . . "Well?"

"It's not only possible," began Stefany . . . "it happens all the time," finished Nataly.

"If I can communicate with home, why don't I get to go home now?" Grace was having a hard time controlling her emotions. She had lost track of whether it was day or night back home. She didn't know how long it had been since she was in this underworld, let alone when she had reached Legba nation with the twins. She had lost all notion of earth time whatsoever. Her body really needed some rest. But she couldn't allow this conversation to stop, yet was so terribly afraid of what the twins would say next.

"The quicker you get a grip on your passage here, the quicker you will be going home. So instead of clogging your thoughts with so much emotion, why don't you just give in to what you will finally know to be right?"

While Stefany was talking, Grace was consciously slowing her bodily rhythm: she began breathing deeply, inhaling and exhaling through her nose; she corrected her posture by straightening her spine, permitting her to breath into a deeper part of her lungs. Before Stefany had spoken, she knew what the twin was going to say. She knew her intuition and clairvoyance were in high gear. Grace got the feeling that she was really alive, and was now one-step ahead of the game.

"How then, do you propose I contact a trusted person back home?" Grace asked the twins.

"You will, quite simply, visit them during their dreams. The sacrifice must be performed by a high level initiate mounted by Danto and offered in your name." Grace had heard enough. She needed time to think alone to regroup and get some rest.

After a moment of uneasy silence, Grace broke the ice:

"Well, that's quite a wild dream I'll be sending home!" She joked,

"I need to think about whom I can trust with this unusual mission, and I think you're right: I do need some rest. Let's take this up again tomorrow, if it's ok with you."

"Sure, of course" both Naftalys answered and stood up.

"If you need anything, just let us know. Please feel comfortable in our house, think of it as your home away from home for as long as you like."

12

THE OTHER SIDE OF REALITY

"Being careful isn't cowardly."

I stood up and left the room headed for the bathroom, and then decided to walk to the kitchen; a quick look around and no one was in sight. How difficult could it be to warm some water without attracting attention? This was my challenge.

An empty pot sat on the small gas stovetop—just my luck. The bottled water was on the counter; I quickly poured a cupful into the pot. Rats! I was going to need matches to light the flame. When I heard footsteps, I hurried in circles and then quickly struck a pose leaning on the counter, trying to look casual and relaxed. False alarm, the steps went away from the kitchen and out the door. I frantically looked around the kitchen for some matches. All I could find was an old lighter out of gas. I couldn't heat the water until I lighted the flame. Frustrated, I quietly walked back to the room where Joel was staying.

I noticed that my friend was very jumpy when I reached the room. I checked his forehead for a fever: nothing. His head was as cool as a clay water jug. I gently ran my fingers through his hair; he was kinda cute, I had to admit; if he weren't so intense, it would be easier to consider him more than a friend. "At times, Joel suffocates me, wanting to get too close too fast, and I didn't like the feeling," I thought aloud, a bit startled by the sound of my voice. Lost deep in the world of disturbing thoughts, I didn't hear Mrs. Majis come in the room.

"Canela." The soft sound of her voice took me by surprise; I turned and looked in her direction. She glanced at Joel then at me,

"Is he your friend?" I nodded my head in agreement. She looked at me obliquely, lowering her eyes self-effacingly.

"Did you want some tea?" I tried not to show my astonishment, simply answering, "Yes, please."

"Should I bring it in a cup?"

"I'll come and get it," and I walked to the kitchen with her.

"What kind of tea should I fix?" was the woman's logical question, and I had to think of an answer quickly.

"I have some of my own," I replied, sounding casual and letting the idea sink in. I watched her light the gas top with the old lighter. I took the round seed from around my neck and held it in my hand. When she handed me the steaming cup I let it fall into the hot water with a plunk, never making eye contact.

Mrs. Majis followed me into the room.

"Do you think he's been poisoned?" Her question worried me. In response to my look of puzzlement, she explained,

"Everybody knows the waree seed you just put in the cup is a powerful anti-poison, even a city girl like you; and if your friend had hemorrhoids you'd put a waree in his pocket." I didn't know much about Majis' wife, but she seemed to know too much for my comfort. I decided I didn't like that, and chose not to answer her question. She didn't let this discourage her, instead came back at me with more.

"How did he take the poison? It's important to know this in order to determine what kind of treatment he needs." The more direct her questioning, the less I wanted to answer. I decided to stick to evasiveness to get her off my back.

"I don't know that he got poisoned . . . I'm just trying to give him something that may help while waiting for the doctor to get here." After this, she realized she wasn't going to get any information from me.

"Well, are you going to give him the tea or not?" She asked before walking over to him and lifting his shoulders off the bed so that he could drink. Of course, I was! I brought the cup to Joel's lips to help him drink. He didn't fight it and even took a few good sips. Settling him back down, she told me to follow her in an imperious tone that didn't accept to a challenge.

We crossed the foyer and went through a hall, where several doors opened onto bedrooms, until we reached the last closed door. She pulled a key from her pocket and entered it in the keyhole saying:

"Have you ever seen a zombie?" before pushing the door open onto a dark room.

When my eyes adjusted to the dim light, I noticed the only furniture in the room was a bare mattress on a metal single-bed frame. Stenches of urine and sweat filled my nostrils. Mrs. Majis crouched down to look under the bed. She pulled me in closer and I watched cautiously. Then she began to sing:

> ♫ *Pierre you have called me from my home, your home is my temple. Pierre Danbala your home is my temple* ♪. *And she put her knee to the ground, dropped her head lower and sang again,* ♫ *Pierre you have called me from my home, your home is my temple. Pierre Danbala your home is my temple.* ♪

She put her right hand under the bed and pulled out a hand moving to the sound of her voice. Then I saw an arm attached to the hand, followed by a shoulder that was slithering on the floor. Next, I made out the head, attached to a twisting neck, chest and body coiling from under the bed. I froze. She stopped singing but the body continued to wind on the floor like a human sized snake. I turned into candy, lost control and peed in my pants.

The "snake" was a small, slim man with dark gym shorts and a loosely fitted, light color muscle shirt. Still as a tree, I had grown roots in my spot, watching as he snaked around the room until he wiggled himself around her and stopped.

"Pierre," said Majis' wife, as he lay there. *"I have a visitor for you today."* He just sat there.

"She knows about poisons and is keeping secrets." My heart was beating so hard I could feel my hair vibrate.

"What do you think we should do, Pierre?" Pierre grunted, "If that's what you want me to do, then that's what I'll do." Mrs. Majis stood up and Pierre took that as a signal. He weaved, turned, and curved his way back under the bed. Like concrete I was cement.

"After you," she said pointing me to the door; I skidded out before her, lost my stiffness and zoomed away like a Ferrari through the hall and back to the foyer. I was relieved to see it was unchanged. I felt like I had stepped into a horror movie and was afraid I could be trapped. I hurried to the room where Joel was resting, Mrs. Majis was right on my heels.

To my surprise, he seemed awake; he sat on the bed and blurted out as I came through the door: "I knew she was ok, look at her sleeping quietly on the twin's couch."

I looked to where Joel was pointing and saw no one, just a chair, and a table. "Who are you talking about Joel?" He didn't appear to have heard my question and kept on ranting.

"Grace cannot be disturbed. She doesn't even understand the magnitude of what this represents . . . Going backwards through the cemetery will wake her up! Then she'll know." I couldn't understand what he was talking about; I knew the words but had no context to help me understand. He suddenly got up and continued talking to presences I was unaware of in this room; his words were clear and so was the tone of his voice.

"Anthony thinks she needs to be startled, shaken up a bit, before she comes to her senses. He may be right. The shock will lower her arrogance and she will become more vulnerable, more malleable and can better integrate the learning she receives."

Both Mrs. Majis and I tried talking to him, but he didn't even register the sound of our voices; it was as if his body was here but the rest of him was somewhere else.

I was shit-scare; Joel my steady friend was freaking out. This house had to be haunted because there was a snaking zombie in the other room and now my buddy was zapping. I really needed to leave quickly before I lost what little bit of sense I had left. The worst part is that I didn't even know where I could go, really; Mr. Boulay brought us here, why would he leave us here if it was dangerous? He had given me a lecture about danger; well, talk about delivering me to the house of zombies as a bad idea.

Mrs. Majis calmed Joel down and coached him back to the bed. He let her sit him down and then he turned to his side and fell asleep in a flash, like his power switch had been flicked off.

Mrs. Majis motioned with her head that I should join her outside of the room. I shook my head from left to right over and over: no way! Last time she took me to zombie land—thank you very much, not me, not again! I found the wooden chair and sat down hard to indicate I wasn't going anywhere. So she moved closer to me.

"What drugs did you kids do before coming here?" she hissed through her teeth, barely hiding her anger.

Drugs? I looked at her like she was crazy.

"Drugs!" I sucked in my teeth in disgust, "you're tripping!"

"If you're telling the truth and you didn't take drugs together, then he probably ate the mushrooms alone. How long have you been together?" I thought about it,

"What time is it anyway?"

"Eleven minutes past eleven."

"I guess we've been together the past seven hours."

"Your friend is on a hallucinogenic journey and may never find his way back." Her words plummeted cargo to a pit in my stomach. She let that idea make its way and loosen my tongue.

"Look at his leg, above the right knee; the red mark is where I think he was stung by a poisoned dart." She easily found the reddish area and inspected the wound.

"Were you together when this happened?"

"Anhan."

"So who shot a poisoned dart at your friend?" I thought about what to say and my instincts told me not to give this woman any information, but I gave in because I was afraid for Joel.

"The midget that guards the wòsh sispann." Her horrified eyes whipped back at me.

"You escaped the brownie? You must know magic!"

"I just know how to save myself."

Mme Majis shot back, "Now this changes everything. We're talking about an adult conversation." With those last words, she left the room.

I wasn't sure what to do, but I knew I couldn't abandon Joel; so I just sat on the wooden chair. Luckily, Mr. Boulay, Majis and someone else came shortly after. I heard the car and then overheard bit of conversation between Mrs. Majis and the newcomers. I waited quietly, watching Joel and worried by the fact that that they would be coming into the room eventually.

13

SWEET DREAMS

"Difficult paths will help you catch smart-ass horses."

Grace felt like the Energizer Bunny: she had been going and going and going. She was no wind-up toy though, and that's what she realized once hit the bed; she kicked off her shoes and rolled over. Feeling uncomfortable in a foreign body, and with important new information shocking her mind, she really wanted to think about home. But she was exhausted, and her brain could no longer keep her body awake; before long, she was in deep sleep.

She began to dream almost immediately. Her dream began with the sensation of heat. It was hot and uncomfortable as she faced a full silver moon and lay down on the sand to cool off. The salty, humid sand cringed against her bare skin when she stretched out her arms and legs to absorb every drop of coolness through the pores in her body. She listened carefully to hear the high-pitched swish of sand and salt crystals rubbing against each other. Her thoughts were about her family but her memories had changed.

Images of another time flashed through her mind; she remembered a loving family and a life of privileges. Like a spectator watching a movie played before her eyes, she painfully relived an experience in which she fell for the trick, had been trapped, shackled in chains, and forcibly marched to the water by men with pointy, chiseled teeth. Since then, she wore shackles and chains.

The nightmare became a horror movie when she reached the sea: boat-people journey with many more like her, shackled by irons and stuffed into the belly of a hot, stinking ship by devilish men with stringy hair, pale skin and whips that lashed out without restraint. Because she was a strong and proud Ibo, she survived the inhumane conditions. Her cousin Equiano had taught her to accept the reality of her new nightmare. He had long ago fallen captive to domestic slavery and later been sold to the traffickers whose human merchandise crossed the sea. He was the reason she had not jumped into the water to return with others whose collective suicide allowed them to return to their ancestors. More so than food or drink, Equiano was what kept her alive. When they reached land, though, bad got worse; worse than a prisoner, she was degraded to sub human and sold a slave for life. She never again saw her cousin who did not leave the ship. Oh! How she longed to be home, back in that blissful reality… Grace could relate to this feeling.

Suddenly he was crushing her! He pinned down her thin waist with the weight of his body; one of his hands cupped her noble neck and he held it in a tight vise. She choked because his thumb pressed against the bump in her throat. He attacked her savagely, ripping through her innocence. But she did not move. Too shocked to react, she concentrated on breathing through her nose. Her thoughts slipped away from the horror of the moment, and floated until her conscious self remembered the pointy iron rod by her side. She waited for the right moment to strike. He was going to pay! She had already paid twice. As he finished and his muscles relaxed, she stuck the rod with rage finding a soft spot right below his ribs, and shoved it through his lungs.

She lay under his dead weight a while, soaking in his blood. Bizarre . . . she derived a certain sick pleasure tasting his blood. She waited until he gasped for his last breath, pushing his dead weight aside before plunging the weapon under her left breast, taking her own life. Soon, other slaves from the compound gathered around. To prove their allegiance to the master's wife, they stabbed the girl's body 158 times.

Her spirit hovered over the body, looking down at what had been a beautiful young woman, beaten beyond recognition and left to look like an animal; just how slaves were described: no better than animals.

Grace awoke soaked with perspiration, what a gruesome nightmare! Yet it had been so real. Her emotions were shot; she knew it was a bad dream, but had experienced the events as though she had been in that girl's body. She got up to get a drink of water, and pondered.

She knew it could have been a real person's story, and prayed to God it wasn't a premonition . . . Grace made an effort to recall the lightness of being she had felt in the beginning; and then, the contrasting pain and terror beginning with captivity. Many places, many times over, too many young women experienced this violation of their bodies, this crushing of their dreams, even this loss of life. Grace shuddered although she was hot and then yawned. Her body was still very tired but her mind was full of shocking images and terrible events; how could she relax and fall back asleep? What kind of dreams would await her once sleep took her to the other side and into her unconsciousness? Neither awake nor asleep, nothing seemed to be working for her. She lamented softly to herself while listening to the chirps of a lonely warbler trying to remind the day it was time to begin.

The sun was lazy this morning, so hummingbirds made up *tic tic tic* trills as a wake up song. A few trogons twittered, *toca-loro*, while a red-legged thrush punctured the rhythm like a guitar bass, *chou-ouek, chou-ouek*, the harmony was complete. Timidly, the morning light broke through the darkness.

Grace slipped into the brisk dawn air, savoring the sudden feeling of freshness and freedom it carried. She stretched her arms and neck and breathed in the minty humid air in gulps, trying to forget the evening's vivid and violent dream. The images were painful—even when relived only as the memory of a dream. Although she was frightened of the gore, she knew that blood in a dream was positive because it symbolized victory.

Walking outside, Grace noticed a white gravel path leading to a nearby clearing. The greenery was still wet with dew, but pink light was mingling with the nighttime dark blue and patiently waiting to hang out with the lighter shades of the day sky. She watched amazed as soft mounds of green bushes shook a pair of transparent wings and fluttered off lazily into the horizon. Moving closer to the clearing, curiosity pushed her to explore the water hole the island/insect had left behind. She approached prudently and heard a lovely feminine voice; the melody drew her in. She could not see well in the fog, but could discern water the size of an Olympic pool; it was a natural water hole surrounded with dense rainbow-green plant life.

The singing continued uninterrupted and Grace settled down by a fragrant orange tree to listen. Soft, pure and persistent, each note sounded more like a flute that a voice; Grace localized the sound coming from her left; she took a few cautious steps and stopped. Twenty five feet away was an enormous purple head; she couldn't believe the lovely and delicate melody had come from this singing head! She waited and listened closely, controlling the sound of her breathing; the wonderful melody had never stopped. It had to be coming from the purple head, there was no other presence but orange trees, bushes and ground vegetation.

She saw movement close to the head and identified a body part, like a purple arm or something. Then another, then another and she concluded it was an octopus . . .

"Why don't you come talk to me? Don't just sit there!" She heard the voice and understood the words, but who had talked?

"Come here, Grace, come here towards me!" The voice had come from the purple head!

"Don't be so worried about what I look like; looks can be very deceiving you know . . . " Grace stood up and thought that it was best if she pretended she wasn't afraid.

"I'm glad we have a chance to talk, one on one." The voice chatted on happily.

"I wanted to have a chance to share some thoughts with you."

"Excuse me, how do you know me? Grace asked.

"There is no where you can go in this nation and not be known after last night."

"I don't remember seeing you last night. Are you an initiate?"

"Well, I certainly could be considered at least an initiate, but I didn't make it last night. No, I'm afraid to say . . . But you shouldn't look so worried; everything went well last night, from what I hear." Grace didn't think things had gone well at all, in fact.

"Are you sure you know what happened last night?"

"Your worries are created by your lack of understanding. If a guardian crosses your road he or she may make your journey more difficult, but it is because success comes with a high price. Your true guides and guardians are by your side helping you through this ordeal. When you rely on them, they will shine through. From what I hear you have a pretty heavy-duty mission . . . That makes you a chosen one. "

"Do you mean that I need not worry about Jewouj?" But worried she was.

"Is she a guardian or a mean-spirit?"

"Je wouj is a guardian so are Mapiang and Marinèt; Ezili is the identifiable archetype. Tell me about yourself, you must be a very special person!"

Not especially lucky to be here, thought Grace, but she answered captivated by this mysterious creature.

"I'm just a girl. I have a mom, a dad, a sister, and a brother; I go to school and play volleyball, and I go to the beach for Spring break. That's where I was last before I came here." The purple head ran a leisurely tentacle from her crown to the spot between the ground and the water where the rest of it lay. Grace could actually see its long eyelashes bow graciously like a performer and, frame by frame, they slowly revealed piercing and shiny blue-black eyes.

"Your location on earth is the Caribbean, correct?" Grace nodded her head in agreement.

"Hmmmm! I'm just guessing, but you could be here because of your DNA." Grace thought about what she knew about DNA: human physiological programming of traits that come from both mom and dad. How could mom or dad's kind of hair, color of skin or eyes, and other physical characteristics be responsible for getting her here? That one flew right above her head but she listened as the purple blob continued patiently.

"Human populations in the Caribbean started with the original Americans who crossed land and water to conquer the New World. I'm speaking of the continents on earth called America: North, Central, and South America. Initiates shared knowledge that led adventurous humans to know wind and ocean currents and they set out to conquer the sea. Scientists show that the Caribbean sits at the bottom of a conveyor belt of ocean currents that carried many travelers, sometimes against their will, to that part of the world. The adventurers came at different times and from different civilizations; they knew how to read the stars to guide their way. If on occasion, reaching the Caribbean happened haphazardly, leaving was not as easy and for the same reason: the sea currents. *Agwe* rules this underworld. So, some stayed and joined with the First to make new lives and blend their bloodlines. You, dear child, are most likely a descendant of this noble DNA; I'll bet you have B- blood"?

Recently Grace had found out about her unusual blood type A+B-. What does that have to do with anything she wondered.

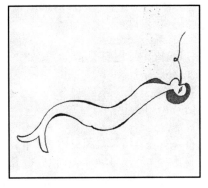

"You will find out that the blood type most prevalent in your area is O but you have a blood type that is found halfway across the world in Africa and the in Middle East. Your body was born in the Caribbean but equipped with DNA from other lands.

"Why would DNA from another place land me here?" Said Grace aloud, hands and arms up in the air showing exasperation.

"Simply put," the purple blob languorously brushed its long lashes, "Knowing very well what legacy they were leaving you, your forefathers arranged for you to come here and get the training you need to be ready to face your destiny."

Ayizan had told Grace to trust her destiny; the twins talked about a zetwal that sets the course for destiny; and now queen purple was explaining that training here was necessary to face destiny. Destiny is not only in the stars but also dictated by DNA and to face it she had to prepare.

Lost in her thoughts she hadn't noticed the purple head blob moving closer. When Grace looked up it was sitting right next to her, and it wrapped a purple arm around her shoulders. It felt cold and wet but Grace didn't move an inch. She wondered what the blob was going to do next; she was less than half the size of its head therefore she was at the strange creature's mercy. She felt a second tentacle wrap itself around her waist and Grace didn't budge a muscle. The tentacle got more adventurous, slipped around her waist, and slyly made its way under her blouse. Slowly, like a pro following a well-known routine, the soft end of the purple tentacle went under the elastic of Grace's bra. The chilling tip snuggled around her breast and was on its way to the nipple. Grace could take no more without protest.

"She shouted off the top of her lungs. Quickly offended, the purple head picked Grace up with all of her purple arms.

"I'm not cute enough for you? OK, Miss Thing from the Caribbean, GET LOST! Maybe my sister can help you; I have no use for you here!" Saying this the purple blob propelled her in the air higher than the trees and above the water. But what goes up must come down, and Grace came back down and plunged into the middle of the pool.

Feet-first, she plummeted towards the bedrock. Once she felt her feet touch ground she tried pushing off to return to the water surface, but her feet stuck exactly where they had touched. Grace opened her eyes, held her breath and evaluated her surroundings. She had landed in a very luxurious all white bedroom spatter-dashed in shiny shells and lustrous pearls.

"What the . . ." Grace inadvertently let out.

"What do you want?" demanded an impatient feminine voice from behind Grace. Her feet were still stuck; so, she turned her head and the top half of her body to see the speaker. Seated on a small stool facing an ornate white coiffeuse, her fair hostess admired herself in an Empress mirror while brushing her long, fiery hair.

"I'm very sorry to interrupt," Grace answered quickly. "I was thrown into the water against my will." Before she finished her sentence, the stunning creature interrupted casually,

"Ah, I bet my sister got angry and threw you in; what did you do to her?" Grace was ashamed of the situation that had led to her being catapulted in the air.

"No matter whose DNA I share this is *my* body and I'll decide who touches me and when! I don't care what other worlds or nations I'm in." Grace faced ahead and crossed her arms over her chest.

"Very well, Miss Lady heard that loud and clear. Now, can you hand me the comb you see there?" Grace was glued to the same spot.

"Would love to help but I can't move," she replied, pointing to her feet.

"Ah, just take off your shoes; when you want to leave you just put them back on and off you'll go." Grace slipped her feet out of her tennis shoes and sunk her ten toes into the broadloom sandy floor.

She took the mother of pearl comb from the round night table beside the bed and handed it to her hostess. Up close, Grace realized she wasn't in the presence of a woman lost in a world under the sea. This being was human from the waist up, but from the waist down her shapely body ended in a fin. She was a mermaid! No wonder she could breathe underwater, thought Grace. Then she realized that she too was also breathing underwater!

"Come here and sit down next to me, Sweetie, and tell me all about yourself. I've been begging for some company for a while now but no one comes by to visit anymore." Grace looked at the creature suspiciously but felt absolutely no apprehension in its presence; not like when she was with the purple blob that made her feel so uncomfortable. How could they be sisters and so completely different? Grace wondered and took the seat the mermaid offered, watching her run the shiny comb through her shiny red mane. The mermaid carried the conversation alone.

"When on your journey through our world-nations you come to me, you are sent to reflect and seek answers deep within yourself. Symbolically, you were plunged into the pool and sent to me, you must delve into your essence, leaving aside the mundane; deeply woven within the fibers of your core are the answers you seek."

A boy walked in with a tray in his hands, put it down on a nearby golden coffee table and left the room without a word. The mistress of the waters graciously shared her meal of white rice and corn flour pudding and a drink of orgeat. Later on, a younger boy came to take away the remains; he too left silently.

"I'm going to tell you about your hair. It just might help you understand. Your beautiful short and fuzzy hair, often called kinky hair, is a characteristic of the people who claimed Earth. You will find that DNA strand has left markers in most of the major racial groups all over the world." Grace pensively ran her fingers over her short bush.

"When I look at you however, I realize that you have other races mixed in, traits like your height betray genes belonging to another group. The remains of the claimers show that they were very small and short especially when compared to you."

Most other girls in her class were short when compared to Grace; she had been the tallest in her class since sixth grade.

"I would guess that the noble arrogance you are so quick to pull out would come from royal ancestry. Such a noble Caribbean people existed once; their name was the Arawak. Come to think of it, they were also known for their curly wooly hair." The mermaid beckoned her to come closer so that she could touch her hair. Grace was going to comply with her request but first asked politely,

"My name is Grace, may I know yours?" The amused mermaid gently put the comb in her hair and began to sing,

> ♪ *Lasiren* ♪ *Labalenn my hat fell into the ocean, I was wooing Lasiren when my hat fell in the sea; I was dallying with Labalen and my hat fell into the sea* ♪ *Lasiren* ♪ *Labalen my hat fell into the ocean* ♫.

"I'm Lasiren and you already met my sister, Labalen."

The soft strokes of the comb reminded her of much simpler times. It had been so long since Grace had seen her family. For whatever the reason, Grace's emotions rolled down her face in the form of warm tears.

14

𝒫ᴜɴɪꜱʜᴍᴇɴᴛ ɪɴ 𝒫ᴀʀᴀᴅɪꜱᴇ

"You can run from the rain and fall into the river."

I must have fallen asleep waiting for the adults to come into the room. I was fast asleep and didn't wake up on my own; Joel quietly tapped my shoulder and immediately put his finger across my lips, motioning to keep quiet. He silently signaled for me to follow him before we crept out a side door, sneaking out into the salt morning dusk.

Joel walked ahead of me quickly, and I had to hustle to keep up with his stride; we continued in silence along the main road for a while. Advancing car headlights forced us into the denser vegetation, where we took shelter under a miniature palm tree. Side to side, we sat motionless until the car and its lights had long passed.

I wondered if Joel had noticed the thumping of my pounding heart; I sure couldn't hear anything else. He cautiously put his hand on top of mine, covering mine within his much larger one. He brought both hands to his chest and set them on his heart. A hard, rhythmic boom-boom-boom was poking through his rib cage. I turned my head toward him and smiled; our eyes connected before, hesitantly, we inched toward each other. Soon our lips pressed in a tender, slow kiss. A rooster crowed in the distance. Joel's lips were dry and, strangely enough, this reminded me of the episode he had the night before. I pulled back my head.

"Joel, what the hell happened to you last night? Do you know?"

Joel knew what had happened. The dwarf had taken sadistic pleasure in explaining to Joel that he would be having recurring hallucinations brought on by the amanita mushroom poison injected with the dart. He could tell Canela this much . . .

"I was poisoned with a dart when we ran into the evil gnome. The poison causes hallucinations—very strong ones—two to three hours after it enters the human blood stream."

Anhan! Mrs. Majis knew about these hallucination, which is why she had asked about drugs.

"Will it come back?" I asked, preoccupied.

"Until the poison completely leaves my system, I will probably have hallucinations again." Joel gently ran the back of his index finger on my cheek; "so we're probably not done, yet . . . But I also know that we had to leave that house as quickly as possible."

I had flashbacks of the previous evening. "Man you don't know half of it! While you were zapping out, Mrs. Majis forced me to a backroom where she keeps a zombie. You hear me? A freaking snake zombie!" Joel looked at me as if he totally understood the fear I had experienced the night before. His eyes went deeply into my soul and touched where I yearned to feel tenderness and friendship; he kissed me again with his still-dry lips , so I licked them softly, playfully and we both laughed.

Snuggled in their penthouse, nestled high up in the royal palm trees, noisy Palmchats tried to shake the clouds off the sleepy sun, *kèk-kèk-kèk-kèk*. Even so, the cold morning sun didn't break through the opaque sky. We wanted to get to the beach and to the island beyond as soon as possible. Joel told me he'd explain everything along the way, mentioning that he actually knew where Grace was and how we were going to meet with her.

We kept to the shadows of the main road. The ocean was within view but more than a couple miles away. I wanted to ask Joel about Grace and what he had seen, but he wasn't very communicative and I was still recovering from the two kisses that I had shared with him. Just the thought of that, kissing Joel, was totally wild! This adventure had taken me way beyond my imagination, for sure. I worried what I was supposed to do if he started having hallucinations again; what if he became uncontrollable!?

"Joel, I'd like you to tell me what I'm supposed to do if you pass out again," I asked; my question remained unanswered. Finally, we approached a clearing with several dugout canoes set upside down, one on top of the other. He pulled me aside to answer my question.

"You should know that the hallucinations are not dangerous, and there is nothing we can do but wait for the flashbacks to end. So, to avoid useless questions, you must find a place where I am safe and no one sees me." Just then, a figure emerged from between two piles of canoes; the person had been asleep and had obviously just awoken. Joel and I both looked at him incredulous, HATUEY! We shouted in unison.

He seemed dazed and reacted in slow motion. Joel made his way around the dugout canoes, but Hatuey didn't seem to recognize him until he was in his face. I watched as they greeted each other, understanding the gist of their conversation following their hands and gestures from a distance. When Hatuey looked in my direction, I waved hello and smiled, not pressed at all to join them. For some reason, he made me uncomfortable; he was always nice and I had no reason to feel that way, but I was uneasy around him anyway. Maybe it was because he was much older and this made me feel inadequate. He was just so tall, handsome, and self-assured. After a few minutes, Joel gestured for me to join them, which I did begrudgingly.

"Hey, Hatuey!" He responded with a nod and a smile, offering a fist so I could tap his in a friendly gesture.

"Hatuey says he last saw Grace yesterday. He ran into her dancing alone in the rarah, so he joined her and they danced together until they reached the beach; then she literally disappeared; she simply slipped into an invisible hole as she set foot into the sea." He had been looking for her ever since. Hatuey looked truly dumbfounded.

Joel explained to Hatuey that he thought we should go to the island to find Grace and convinced him to join us. Grace's friend had no better plan, so he readily agreed. They suggested we find some fruit or something to eat on the beach, and cross the water while the tide was low.

I had a soft banana and a not-so-ripe mango and I was good. The guys had to have more and helped themselves to ripe, yellow-green avocadoes buttered on crunchy cassava bread. They washed it down with AK100, a local drink made of mashed soaked-corn slowly cooked in water. I was impatient. I didn't understand; how could Grace have disappeared and slipped into thin water? She just had to be on the island . . . She really just had to be there! If not, where could she be?

It was time to get going, but the two of them were taking their own sweet time. I wondered how they could consume so much food. If I ate like that, I'd be as big as a cow; Joel was slim and Hatuey was slimmer. Life isn't fair!

After too long, we took to the clear water; it was cool and stung my skin. We were moving slowly, even though it was no more than four feet deep. Hatuey and Joel talked while I lagged behind, inattentive to what they discussed. I swam for a while underwater, close to the bottom, challenging my lungs to withstand long periods without coming up for air. When I started hearing the thumps, I thought it was blood rushing to my ears because of the exerted effort. I came up for air and was about to go right back under until I heard Hatuey call my name.

"Canela!" His tone was urgent; I stopped immediately and opened my eyes. It took a moment to blink out the salty water before I saw Joel in his arms. Oh shit! It was happening again! Hatuey looked at me desperately. Glancing at the island and at the beach, I estimated we were half way between both options, we quickly agreed to take him to the island.

Gosh, now I was going to have to talk to Hatuey alone! I panicked and blurted out that a dart had poisoned Joel; no matter how true, my story sounded far-fetched. Maybe I shouldn't have started talking about the dwarf. Hatuey looked at me like I was crazy. Finally, I shut up and kept swimming. I left Hatuey to take care of Joel, now easily floating on top of the water as our friend attended to him.

Exiting was trickier; Hatuey wrapped Joel's left arm around his neck and over his shoulder, and instructed me take the right side. We quickly walked up the beach between some leafy miniature palms, and set our friend on the sand to rest in the shade of an almond tree.

15

A PEARL, A MIRROR AND A TRUMPET

"Lightning bugs shine for themselves."

Grace had fallen asleep, her head on Lasiren's lap, and that's where she awoke. The mermaid's gentle strokes were comforting. For some reason, she felt comfortable and trusted the curious creature. Lasiren would help Grace realize that she couldn't fight her way out of this predicament, which she had to accept and absorb. The gatekeeper understood this change would happen in the young woman she was watching sleep peacefully.

"Grace," the mermaid whispered, "I want to help you find your way. I have keys to open closed doors, and I can give you clues to guide you on the path to success." Grace listened to the message knowing that there would be strings attached.

"All I ask," said the mistress, "all I want . . . is for you to remember us now and cultivate this relationship we started here together."

Grace remained quiet; she was thinking about Ayizan. That gatekeeper had also offered to help whenever she needed her; all she had to do was to find a royal palm tree and call upon her friend. That seemed less compromising; Lasiren was asking for more, the promise of a lasting relationship, which would go beyond this place and follow her home . . . if she ever found her way there. But alone, Grace doubted she could ever find her way; she couldn't even tell if she was any closer to leaving here or not. Deep down, she knew she needed help. Ayizan had told her to follow her instincts, which were telling her to trust Lasiren. Even if she called upon Ayizan later on, there were neither palm nor gum trees in Lasiren's room and she had to leave here first.

"One thing is for sure, I won't forget you, that is, if I ever get to leave this world-nation. I wonder if you're lonely here and I understand you want some friendship and company. I can only promise what I know I can deliver; first you must tell me what my obligations will be." Lasiren smiled at her newfound friend's brazen astuteness.

"Friendship, like most relationships, consists of give and take; you must put in to take out. I offer gifts that make you powerful and grant special magical abilities such as disappearing or vanishing in thin air. However, you have mistaken friendship for loneliness. The last thing I need is a visit from arrogant young people who have lost their world! Now I know why my sister catapulted you into the water."

She sprung upright, barely giving Grace the time to remove her head. When she crossed the room, the facets of the diamonds in her long white skirt caught and reflected light like a disco ball. Captivated by the scintillating rainbow, Grace didn't notice Lasiren's exit; but knew immediately when the mermaid had departed, for she was now in utter darkness.

Spooked, Grace stayed put. Footsteps entered the room and she guessed the shape of a child carrying a dim light; a second and then a third, each carried a conch shell and from its center filtered a luminous glow. They placed themselves in a triangle around her and sat on the floor, setting the shell light in front of them. Grace wasn't sure what to do or say; at first, they spoke no words. Then each recited a verse of this poem:

> *Three brothers crossed Three Rivers stepping through time*
> *Too happy but unlucky was their only crime*
> *At the stroke of three, indeed, the bells did chime*
> *The current swirled and swallowed them into the paradigm...*
> *Release them and together your powers will combineIlluminate from*
> *within and connect to your divine*

Grace wondered what the poem meant . . .

"How can we get out of this place? Does any one know?" Grade demanded.

The smallest boy stood up conch lamp in hand. "I know the way, let's not waste time."

Grace stepped back into her shoes and followed.

Only the first shell had a light; they moved ahead in semidarkness. Grace felt as if an electrical current were brushing across her face and her heart accelerated. No one talked; they just walked.

Drums resounded in the background and the group proceeded in the opposite direction. The call of a conch shell blanketed them and froze their steps. The smallest brother brought his shell to his lips and blew a lonely note carried by the distance. Behind her, one of the boys tripped, kicking rocks to her heels. She looked down, where a colored broken disc attracted her attention. Something about the saucer part reminded her of her friend Canela; she collected shells and rocks. She picked it up and ran her finger over the chiseled surface and crevices; she then slipped it into her pocket, promising herself to give it to her friend if she ever saw her again.

Shortly thereafter, a school bus pulled up alongside them; it was hard to tell its color because it had no lights.

"*Savalwe papa Pierre.*" Each brother greeted the driver as he boarded the bus. The driver looked at Grace: "So whas-it gonna be? You hoppin' on girl or stayin' behin'?" She stared at the small man's round head, surprised by his shiny noggin, before stepped onto the bus.

"Greetings" she addressed him with a discrete smile, before moving to the back towards a seat. Besides her traveling companions, there was only one older man sleeping in the back of the bus. Grace found a spot next to the oldest brother and plopped down. A vinegar smell filled the bus as it took off.

"So where does this bus take us?" The question was routine, although the boy didn't answer immediately,

"I'll make it this time, and I know I'm ready," Declared the boy who did talk but never seemed to answer her questions. So Grace asked where they were headed once again. For a while, only silence was her answer, and it hung still in the air with the vinegar cloud.

"Prepare and be ready," bellowed a voice from the back. "You are on your way to the land of the dead and that's the only way to get out alive." A stunning man came to his feet, and in one sweeping motion draped his red cape over his shoulders.

"Let me off at the next stop, Pierre. I'm not taking this group to Takwa; they'll have to make this journey on their own." His sentence took him to the front of the bus, next to the driver.

"This is not good," the youngest commented to the brother next to him. "We need all the help we can get and now Angelo's leaving; this is not good!"

"Well," my seat companion thought aloud, "maybe it's best he go. We haven't succeeded getting into Takwa nation yet, and he's been with us the past twenty times we've tried. I say good riddance . . . Let him go! I bet I can get us through better than he can. Besides," pointing to Grade, "she is with us, so we're sure to succeed; it was foretold." His voice sounded like a premonition.

Grace had registered the conversation and the "twenty tries" part stuck in her mind.

"You kids have tried to get out of here twenty times already!?" Again, her question was to no one in particular. Surprisingly the middle brother finally said something.

"And this is our last chance."

"What do you mean your last chance?"

"There are magical numbers here: 3, 6, 7, 9 and 21. To get out you must hit upon one of these numbers. This will be our twenty-first try. The next chance we might get is 120; everyone we knew will be dead by then." My! The gravity of this attempt carried a frightful finality.

"Why did you fail to get in the past times?" she wondered.

"There's a bouncer named Linto at the door; he's a mean bastard, but he knows his job. He is to let no one in until it's time. No one. No exceptions. And he makes no mistakes, period."

The discussion between Pierre and Angelo got louder. Angelo stormed toward the back of the bus, "Which one of you stole Anoli?" he roared. "You better give it back," he bullied them, shaking his index finger.

"Thunder and lightening!" He barked kicking his rage into a seat. "You give me my lizard or I'm coming to get it and I won't stop until I find it; I don't care if I have to undress the four of you!" He crossed his arms, squared his stance, and waited. The two boys in the front seat stood up, pulled off their tee shirts, and turned their short pockets inside out. Grace's companion stood and did the same. She felt ashamed. No way was she going to pull her tee shirt off in front of everybody! She hadn't stolen anything; she didn't even know what this man was talking about.

"How about you, young lady?" Inquisitive eyes locked on hers, shooting sparks that demanded an answer.

"I don't know what you're talking about . . ." Grace shrugged her shoulders and lifted the palm of her hands upward, a gesture to indicate she knew nothing.

"Stop this bus! I'm taking the girl; she's going to give me back what is not hers to keep." The bus came to a halt and Pierre opened the back door. Angelo told Grace to get off the bus. She was scared and didn't want to go. Her companion pushed her off the seat.

"Go, get out of here, hurry and give him back his lizard if you know what's good for you. You better make it quick if you want a chance at getting out of here."

Angelo yanked her hand, forcing her to stand, and then shoved her off the bus. The door slammed behind them.

She was blind, in the dark again. It felt like they were in the middle of a forest; Angelo started walking away but Grace didn't move. Maybe they were inside of a cave, she thought, because she could discern vertical shapes around them; perhaps they were stalagmites or stalactites, she wondered.

"Come on girl, we don't have all day! Follow me." She realized she had no choice, so she followed along. She had to walk closely behind him in order not to be lost in the pitch blackness.

Angelo came to a stop before a structure and Grace stood behind him.

"Papa!" he called out. Then he stomped his walking stick three times. A door slid open onto a well-lit foyer. Angelo knocked on the entrance once, twice then a third time. "Papa . . . "

Bright lights immediately blinded Grace, once inside. She heard conversations that were well underway before she was able to visually take-in her environment. Angelo was talking to a being with many faces. A pretty, oblong mask with dark hair pulled up in a bun crowning an orange head looked straight at her. In place of ears, the being had other heads. On the left side was a profile that resembled a Greek statue. On the immediate right was a mime, next to a red devil with three horns and last, a mango shaped profile; two bubble-looking planetary objects gravitated around its slender neck. The shock came when Grace looked at its chest and saw an ear above an eye in place of the heart! She trembled when she realized that the eye had been scrutinizing her all along! It felt like it was evaluating her, reading the depths of her soul. Good God Almighty, now I've seen it all, she thought. The being motioned Grace to step forward and she took a baby step. Angelo turned towards her.

"This is the young lady and she needs to rest. Can you please show her the guest room?"

"Please follow me" vibrated the melodious tones of a deep voice. It matched the body and the multi-faced head; strangely enough, the rather unusual combination was well proportioned and its manners gentle. They walked in silence down a long hall lined in colorful primitive paintings and stopped in front of a wooden door. The door swung gently and creaked open onto a small white room. A futon bed was in the center and was the only piece of furniture. On the floor next to the bed were a notebook and pencil.

"It will be helpful if you write your dreams there when you awake."

"But, I'm not sleepy!" Grace tried to protest, but the door closed and locked shut before she finished her sentence.

What a drag . . . Panicking would get her nowhere; screaming her lungs off wouldn't either. She felt frustrated and wanted to cry, but she didn't. What would be the use? It would not get her any further . . . no closer . . . nope, crying wouldn't help one bit. Besides, it would make her feel even sorrier for herself. Grace had succeeded in getting to the second gate with Ayizan's blessing.

She hadn't fared as well in Legba nation, however; this was for certain! Legba had said he would refuse to talk to her until she took care of the unfinished business. She left without even thanking the twins; she was sure Labalenn, and Lasiren would have no kind words for her either. Now locked up inside the earth, a multi-headed being wanted her to go to sleep and record her dreams!

Grace needed some help. So, right hand to her forehead, then to her chest, left shoulder and, lastly, right shoulder, she protected herself with the sign of the cross. Baptized and raised Catholic, she very naturally began to recite the Our Father. It calmed her, so she recited the Hail Mary, and then she continued with the Credo. Then, she decided to confess so that regardless of what happened next she was at peace with God. She fell asleep at some time during her confession, but not before feeling some regret for her arrogance toward Lasiren.

Surrendering to her fatigue and the comfort of the bed, she entered REM sleep right away. Grace dreamed she stood prisoner in the middle of a circle composed of everyone she had met in these world-nations so far. Her accuser was Angelo, of course; he wanted to prove to the others that Grace had taken Anoli, his pet lizard. Ayizan, ever her ally, was the first entity to speak.

"If she really has it, then, we will find it on her person. Young lady take off your blouse!" Her tone was imperative and Grace obeyed and removed her top.

Rozalen was beside Ayizan and her turn came next.

"How do you know that Grace is the one who took your lizard?" Her question was formulated in defense of her friend.

"To begin, I've taken the boys to Lakwa twenty times and this has never happened before. Next, all the boys stood, removed their shirts and emptied their pockets; she is the only one who didn't volunteer."

"So empty your pockets girl and make the man happy!" Grace was happy to see her friend again and wanted to talk to her, but she felt a sharp poke at her side. To her amazement, Hatuey was the one with the devil's fork.

"Hatuey!" She gasped. He poked her harder gritting through his teeth.

"Do what Rozalen says and be quick," he instructed. Grace's blood took a turn and she thought she could explode, she was so furious. But this was a dream and she was aware of that, so she decided it was best to play the game. She emptied her pockets for everyone to see. Out came the piece of the broken red disk she had picked up, but no lizard came out crawling.

"See!" She grinned.

"Silence!" hissed Hatuey. She raged inside but said not a sound came out.

The twins were next and she braced to hear their comments.

"A person who disregards common courtesy," started Nataly, and Stefany continued, "one who will sleep in your bed and wear your clothes and not even thank you is an ingrate, capable of anything. Just strip her of her pants and we will see where she has hidden the little critter."

Grace unzipped her jeans and pulled them off. No Anoli! She was now standing in her underwear facing her judges. Labalen was next and Grace knew nothing good was to come.

Labalenn began with a soft chuckle that built into a belly up laugh; she suddenly snapped. "So you were cute? Tsk! So you thought you were better than me, huh? Well, laughs the best she who laughs last. Take off that bra and let me see your boobies . . . I've been curious about what they look like." Grace knew better than to resist. She slipped the straps off, slid the bra around, and unhooked; then she let the bra drop to the floor; the ankh Ayizan had given her hit the ground first.

Lasiren was next and Grace knew she would have her take off her panties. So she didn't even wait for the mistress to talk; she slipped the panties off one leg after the other.

"One of your strongest qualities is your intelligence. You've done well, but you're missing a step. Now, kneel to the ground," and Grace did just that.

"OK, lean to the front as if you were bowing in adoration or prayer." Grace followed her instructions.

"Ladies and gentlemen, observe the thief . . . Grace, spread your legs." Reluctantly, Grace moved her legs. "Come on girl, you can do better than that," snapped Labalen. Grace was afraid to open her legs because she could already feel the small creature crawling on her pubic hair. It felt like it had crawled right out of her belly button. The lizard dropped and wriggled on the floor in plain view for all to see.

"Snatch a catch!" cried Angelo, "I knew she was the culprit. Drag her to the altar!" he ordered.

Grace crawled on her knees to the corner of the room where brilliant colored paintings and decorated images of saints surrounded a boat with the words *Ife Imamou* inscribed on the side. Leaning against the wall, and competing for space on a small table, was a fantastic array of objects—flags, kabalistic pottery, bells, magical weapons, rosaries, necklaces, books, stones, skulls, a sword, and even drums. Angelo made her lay flat on the ground, face down, with her head facing the altar. Next, he doused her three times with water. Drums began to rumble in the background. Grace's heart stopped.

"You have one chance left," Angelo softened. "You must make the right choice or loose everything."

At that precise moment, Grace woke up

16

JOEL'S TRIP

"God's pencil has no eraser"

The *amanita muscaria* mushroom contains a number of hallucinogenic chemicals: ibotenic acid, muscimol, muscazon and muscarine. Eating the mushroom can lower your blood pressure, cause nausea, twitching, drowsiness, visual distortions, mood changes, euphoria, and hallucinations. In near fatal doses it may even cause madness characterized by bouts of mania alternating with quiet hallucinations.

The gnome's mushroom distillate was a potent concentrate of the drug. He had prepared his special formula with ill intent, going so far as to dip the points of his darts several times to coat mega doses of the chemical; he fantasized about a lethal dose every time he hit a victim. This time it had been Joel—a wrong place, wrong time kind of thing.

Actually, Joel was lucky because he had felt no nausea, and the dose wasn't strong enough to produce madness; so, most of the time, when he looked like he was sleeping, he was hallucinating. His hallucinogenic trips echoed many themes of his life. He felt like a passenger in a video rollercoaster, stuck in another reality, watching a three-dimensional recording of life. During his ride, his path crossed others' lives; they also were on life-ride learning lessons that helped them to cope better with their earth reality. He would have benefited even more greatly had he been able to remember everything he was experiencing in this short time. But the time frame was too short for him to process or totally absorb the depth of the emotionally rich experiences. He would forget many of the details and even some of the events; but he would retain the most important lessons and sometimes details long forgotten would pop up later on in dreams.

The chemicals in the mushroom caused the line between his consciousness and unconsciousness to blur; the usual parameters of time and space on earth were distorted. Joel's ability to distinguish between himself in the present and his place in the cosmos was altered. Walking in the water to the island had sent him traveling onto another thread of time when a distant relative had crossed this same spot back in another time.

Byblos is the name of the oldest city in the world, which goes back at least 9000 years. Byblos gave its name to the Bible and it is the birthplace of the first linear alphabet. Sidon is perhaps the second oldest city and its inhabitants founded Tyre. Joel's ancestor was a native son of Tyre.

History recorded the voyages of a great navigator of Tyre known as Cadmus, who left his city – Cadamiat – on a mission to study the Cuchite language spoken in Brazil. Joel's hallucination connected him to the energy of his distant relative, the young Melqart, Son of Baal of Tyre, who was among the captain's guests.

As was the custom thousands of years ago, Cadmus' ship, the *Carpássios*, traveled between the Brazilian coastline and the Caribbean. The second largest of the islands, the one the locals called Kiskeya, was internationally renowned for its precious woods and valuable amber. Melqart waited impatiently from behind the seahorse starboard, watching as they sailed into the limpid-blue beaches brushing against the blond sand, closely guarded by thick vegetation that carpeted the land and covered mountains behind mountains. He appreciated the luxurious morning landscape with the eyes of a connoisseur in the wood trade. Setting foot on this island would mean the realization of his dreams to discover new places with exotic lumbers that would serve to expand the family's cedar wood business.

He jumped into the crystalline water in full attire. Many locals had already come up small dugouts, *boumbas,* to greet the visiting group. He reveled in the warmth of the tropical ocean and in the friendly people who welcomed him to their island. They would become the Taino—people of goodwill— and Arawak—noblemen. Their welcome party's joy in spying their visitors came from previous contacts in which they had exchanged amber, gold, and special cotton cloth for purple dye, glass beads and intricately embroidered cloths. Taino shamans and the traveling healers would exchange secrets and healing leaves and medicines. The indigenous population knew the people of the Seahorse boats well, and the relationship had always been mutually profitable. Melqart loved everything he saw about this place, especially the happy, bare-chested native women who had come to greet him. They spoke strange sounds, giggled, smiled, and held his hands. Three sun-baked bronze young women placed necklaces of shells strung on fiber rope. *Bejucos* they said while their dexterous hands fondled his neck. Melqart thanked them with his blinding smile and filled their hands with glass beads from his pockets.

Joel lived through this experience as if he were Melqart; this reality registered in both of their consciousnesses simultaneously but in perfect symbiosis. They had connected through Earth energy, meaning Joel could ride this burp in time, slipping in and out of both realities unpredictably. Especially because Melqart's journey was so enjoyable, it was hard for Joel to resist the temptation of wanting to become Melqart permanently.

The young women took Melqart inside a *bohio*, a Taino house, where a feast awaited. Cadmus had told him stories of the Taino people's wonderful hospitality, but this went way beyond his expectations. His seat was special and set aside. The locals called it a *duho*, a four-legged stool made from precious wood with ornate relief and concave carvings. The dark mahogany was like nothing he had ever seen before. How had they treated the wood to obtain this color? They couldn't have imagined what this event meant to him! Above all else, he wanted to meet the person who could take him to see wood like this, but language was a barrier. Unable to further his curiosity he took part in the celebrations at hand.

Food and music, poetry and dance—the Taino were showing their guests the complexities of their culture and the richness of their rituals. Melqart knew enough about court protocol to realize that his seat was an important symbol. Few people had duho seats, and those besides the guests who did had rich attire, feathers in their hair, colorful decorations on their bodies and with people serving their every need. He knew they were the leaders and that meant he was an honored guest.

A man not much older than him drew his attention; multi-colored feathers crowned his noble, flat forehead. High cheekbones and a chiseled nose reminded him of a barn owl with a heart-shaped face. Melqart watched as they handed him a Y-shaped object that he took into both hands. After applying the top of the Y to each his nostrils, he inhaled and then removed the object and blew smoke out of his nose and mouth. The young Phoenician had already partaken in this practice in Brazil, the stop before this one; he understood that these similar looking indigenous tribes shared some beliefs, rituals, and practices. The young leader had also noticed Melqart watching and sent a servant to invite the Phoenician to join him.

They spoke through a local translator. The host welcomed his visitor, offering to share his smoke. Melqart graciously accepted; because of prior experience, he took small controlled breaths and managed not to cough or choke. This impressed the *cacique*, the local chief; few foreigners were able to inhale the cohoba smoke; even fewer knew how to act while under the influence. Melqart appeared in control, even seeming to enjoy the celebrations which helped gain the cacique's respect. After a while, Melqart diplomatically approached the subject of the wood. He learned that for the Taino people wood was a more valuable commodity than gold. Despite that, he obtained the cacique's approval to visit the place where trees that produced dark wood grow. To settle the agreement they smoked more cohoba, a means for them to communicate with the spirit world—so the Taino believed. Melqart didn't mind the practice, he preferred the spirits be in favor of all their undertakings and he enjoyed the smoking.

The cacique explained that the Taino envisioned the cosmos round and sliced into three horizontal layers: the celestial vault on top, the earthly plane in the middle and the subterranean waters on the bottom. In the beginning, the spirits kept the three world layers together by weaving designs and symbols into a magically interconnected net that connected all things on Earth. Only the spirit of the dead could remain in constant communication on all three planes. Among the living, shamans were the only ones who would dare wander away from the earthly plane.

The two men, in need of fresh air, wandered from the bohio out to the courtyard, where young women and men were gathered in a rectangular area like a playing field. Two pillars stood vigil at the end of each team's court. Melqart and the cacique stood to the side. The players kept the ball in play by bouncing it off their heads, shoulders, or hips. Team members would pass it to each other until they could try to score, by entering the ball between the pillars at the end of field in the adversary's court. Melqart watched as the teams controlled the ball and distributed passes with precision; both teams appeared equally skilled so he wondered what would determine the winner, each team had scored twice in the opponent's camp.

"How do you know it's over?" Melqart asked the cacique, turning to the translator for an answer. While distracted this way, Melquart did not notice the ball leaving the court and hurtling toward the spectators. But it feel he did when the ball bounced off the back of the head. He hadn't imagined the ball being so hard, and the hit stunned him for a good while.

For Joel the effect was immediate; it returned him back to his body on the Port Salut beach. It was hot; probably the middle of the day, and the greenery under which he lay could no longer offer protection from the heat. Hatuey was asleep next to him, but Canela was nowhere in sight.

Power, wealth, or knowledge?

"She took her bullet in the forehead"

Pierre, the multi-headed being, entered the room on cue as if he had been spying on her. Grace was startled by her dream and suspicious of this "thing" standing at the foot of the bed.

"So, tell me your dream," he demanded.

"Who says I had any dreams?" replied Grace, not missing a beat. She was uncomfortable and locked in this room against her will . . . Damned if she was going to cooperate!

"Listen, you can save the hostility; it's only wasted energy. I don't make the rules here. I'm just the messenger. Do you need some time to collect your thoughts?"

"No . . . don't go!" Grace preferred that Pierre stay; he knew how to get out of this room.

"Well, if you feel ready, we can carry right along." He seemed to be having a good time.

"I'm glad someone's enjoying this adventure." Grace said aloud, although he didn't seem to have heard what she said; this, or he chose to ignore her comment. Instead of responding, he sat on the bed.

"I'm going to tell you a story. I want you to pay close attention and think carefully."

"This story has been recorded by historians and happened on the old continent of Africa during the Mandingo civilization. One day, Emperor Abukari called his three sons and his brother.

"Destiny and 200 ships await us," he explained. "We will undertake a great and perilous voyage. Before we depart, I will give you each a gift. You are free to select your own gift today, but your choice will determine the future, beginning at dawn tomorrow.

Emperor Abukari continued, "I can only give you what I have. First, I offer the gift of power. Next, I will gladly bequeath my fortune. Lastly, I will share what I have spent my lifetime acquiring: knowledge."

Following the customs of the time, the oldest son chose first. He took power; the second son picked fortune, which left the youngest with knowledge.

"You are asked to participate and play an interactive role in this story, Grace; which one of the brothers would you like to be?" Grace considered the three choices. She was a team player, that's why she loved volleyball. She considered the option of having power before deciding she would have a hard time being the leader. It's lonely at the top, she thought, having to make all the important decisions. Besides, along with this option came the many obligations; so she decided to pass on this one. Next came fortune; like the second Abukari brother in the story, she was also a middle child and found this choice appealing; and, to her, having a great fortune seemed the best gift of all. She pictured herself on a formidable ship with treasure chests full of gold, gems, and jewels . . . So what was the third choice? She couldn't even remember.

"What did the youngest son get?"

"Knowledge, my dear; he was given knowledge."

"What kind of knowledge does he get?" Pierre was taken aback by her brashness, showing his irritation through his answer to the question.

"All kinds of knowledge! Abukari knew about medicine and healing with plants and remedies, about the seas and the different currents, about the skies and the stars and he had maps on many lands." To Grace, this sounded exactly like the type of stuff you'd want to know to survive 'great and perilous voyages.'

Forget the riches; they're just going to weigh down the ship, Grace remarked to herself. "I want the knowledge if I'm going on a voyage, so I pick to be the youngest." With a quizzical smile, Pierre asked if she was sure that was her choice.

Grace doubted herself and thought through her options again: power, fortune, and knowledge. The context was an upcoming perilous voyage and she could have any of the three. Power would command the respect of everyone around her. Fortune could buy anything she wanted. Knowledge . . . now why was it she wanted knowledge? How many times had her parents told her that what you learn is yours to keep and is knowledge forever, that no one can take it away? The others, both money and power, are ephemeral, and might disappear at any time. Grace felt that knowledge was the right choice in her gut.

"Yes, that's exactly what I want: knowledge."

"Well, if that is your choice I must proceed. I guess I didn't mention magic in the knowledge you would be given. Because of your choice I must now help you open your third eye" He took some white powder in his palm and playing his index against his thumb he let it slide to the ground. "What is that?" Grace was curious.

"Just flour. Now pay attention to the design." He began on the left with the first leaf of a clover shape; then traced the middle and last leaf to complete the three leaf clover. He finished his *veve* by putting an upside down capital V above and then drew two ram horns on each side. He sprinkled a few stars here and there before informing:.

"This is my veve. Since you selected knowledge, you must trace your own." Grace took the silky feeling flour into her right hand.

"Begin with a triangle," instructed Pierre. She traced a triangle.

"Now make a flagpole coming from the base and through the top and center." She finished the flagpole.

"Atop the pole draw three lines that cross the flagpole and make an asterisk like star." Grace made three lines cross the pole to make a star.

"Right below the star, draw the horns for Aries the ram." She traced the curved shape of a horn in one movement.

"From the top of the triangle, start on the left side of the flagpole and write the S of a snake." Grace's snakehead barely touched the end of the ram horn.

"Very good, very good!" Pierre commented.

"Last but not least: call Anoli. It's on you; you know that from your dream. Now you must learn to control it. Concentrate, focus on the animal, and command it to your hand." Grace straightened her spine, breathing slowly through her nostrils, and followed the passage of her breath through her lungs; she visualized the little green lizard.

"Wait a minute, how could you know what I was dreaming about?" Pierre laughed.

"You are a tough cookie! I shall help you understand." Pierre stood up, bringing his hands to his head and multiple faces. Then he pushed the many faces back, revealing a single head and face. Amazing! Grace was shocked and retreated floored . . . Pierre turned around and was a dreamboat.

"Now, you see me as only a few, such as my wife Ayidawedo, have seen me. My multiple heads are to me what your other eye can be for you. It will perfect your ability to see because you it gives you access to another sense, another means to perceive, to evaluate, and even to foresee things . . . that is, if you learn to use your full potential. Each of my faces, as you would call them, is a set of multiple perceptions and powers that belong to different realities; each brings a set of abilities—another pair of eyes, a nose, ears—through which information enters and is processed by the my brain. Within a certain proximity, I can join you and watch you in the realm of dreams through my mime-face. That's why I knew exactly when you were about to awake."

Grace felt somewhat ashamed that Pierre had shared her dream and smiled shyly. She realized that she had won his trust because he had taken off his crown of many faces and was touched that he had shared this space with her. She also realized that he was a being and not a thing.

Grace focused upon the spot between her eyes where Pierre had indicated her third eye; she inhaled and exhaled rhythmically, visualizing the lizard she had seen in her dream. She extended her arm, turned her right palm upward and, low and behold, the little green critter! Grace laughed aloud. She liked the thing immediately and felt a connection, like for a pet. She put it on her breast near her shoulder and ran her fingers from its head to its tail.

"I can see why Anoli picked you." Pierre also laughed and was happy he had coached her to success.

"Dab Anoli in the flour and place the shape on the right, next to the triangle . . . Perfect."

"Now, I will finish the story. Let me tell you about the other brothers. The oldest son who had asked for power did not leave the next day. He had received his father's throne and he stayed with his uncle to rule the entire kingdom.

Son Two arrived at the port before dawn and boarded a ship loaded with riches. They were among the first in the fleet to take to the seas. They set sail off the Guinean Coast and passed the Cap Verde Islands. It was early in the year and the cold air made for a swift North Equatorial Current and the

confident crew navigated the middle of the current. Entering the strong North Atlantic Current, the fleet's first lighter ships drifted further east than anticipated. The weightier vessels upheld the struggle however. No matter how hard they fought, the inexorable force attracted them; the lighter ships went into an area now called the Bermuda Triangle, and no one ever heard of them again. Son number two was lucky to save his life, his ship, and his treasure chests.

First, he secured his treasure; then he reorganized his fleet, addressed his men, and set course on the imaginary line of the Tropic of Cancer, guessing he would soon hit land mass. His calculations were correct and before long he saw land. However, pirates known as filibusters had long ago discovered this area, and they waited in fringing reefs surrounding the islands for such happenstance. This vicious mob of pirates fell upon the battered crew and quickly decimated the already dwindling fleet. Son Two's fabulous treasure chests had found new masters. An unfortunate end came to a once very rich fleet: what the voracious pirates abandoned as waste, the seasonal hurricane winds and torrential rains reduced to smithereens."

To learn the end of the story for the role you picked, you will have to step on the veve you traced and I will help you embark on this trip." He began to sing and the melodious sound came from the Greek looking left side of his head,

♪Osany O, Ain't nothing sweet about being poor, Osany O.♫

Grace stepped on her veve and felt her legs sink into the ground. She locked with the power of the magic symbol, calling upon Anoli just as she had before, and mastered the command. From her hand, she transferred it to her left shoulder.

Just like Anoli on her shoulder, Grace became an invisible lizard on the third son's shoulder, in perfect unison with him while his father scoured the kingdom to collect the plants he would need for his voyage. Before he was allowed to depart, this third son, Abukari3, was made to study Earth and its fauna; he learned about the atmosphere, the sea and air currents. During this intense period of tutelage, he learned how to read the skies and where to look for stars and hidden galaxies. With simple magic and enthusiasm, he devised tricks and retained all of the information. When time came, he calculated the voyage with significant knowledge of currents and seasons. The fleet navigated swiftly and followed a precise course based on *portolano* maps obtained from Arab merchants who charted stars and followed astrological markers.

Up the Guinean Coast, past the Cap Verde Islands, they entered the North Equatorial Current in the beginning of spring and the air was perfect. From there, the entire fleet entered the North Atlantic Current as if on a conveyor belt, moving along effortlessly; it set a southwest sail using the constellation of Orion as point of reference. Moving south, Orion began to shift upward and the Crab Nebula showed a whole cast of new stars. The African's astrological calculations oriented them to where Orion was not quite overhead. At that point, another star appeared in the horizon called Canopus. After traveling a few more weeks, a pair of stars named Alpha and Beta Centauri would appear down low near the southern horizon in the early morning. This would be when the fleet knew it had reached southern skies. The son's calculations and maps did not lie and land mass was close by.

Barbados, Ichowigaim or "big red animal lying on its side" is the eastern-most Caribbean island. It was created less than one million years ago by the collision of the Atlantic and Caribbean plates and a volcanic eruption. This was the land mass first encountered by the fleet, which was greeted by the native population, the war hungry Carib Indians; and they were a savage lot. The Indians let the boats reach the coastline and cast anchor, watching and waiting as the first group of Africans left the ship and entered the water. They calmly allowed the Africans to cover the distance between ship and shore. Only then their bowmen, armed with poisonous arrows, took aim. No African reached the shores alive; Abukari's youngest born was among the first victims.

According to information gleaned by King Abukari about the natives of this island, the people were gentle and welcoming. While once correct the information was outdated by the time Abukari's youngest son came ashore.

The ringed-nose Arawak, *caciques*, and noblemen had also been the victims of the ruthless Caribs, who had invaded the island in the thirteenth century. It was said that the Caribs would consume the flesh of their captives and wash it down with cassava beer.

Grace had traveled on Abukari3's shoulder and Anoli on hers; she was invisible to all and only she knew how to make Anoli appear. She was dependant upon the prince's adventure and traveled through time with him. When his life ended, she accompanied him on his journey to the other side.

Grace was now facing Abukari3 in front of a cemetery. As a woman, she laid eyes on the prince for the first time. He towered more than a head above her; this was unusual and amusing she thought. She noticed her three young friends and the bus driver on the left, by the entrance, waiting.

The youngest saw her and walked in her direction. The prince didn't notice the boy come up to them; he seemed oblivious to his surroundings.

"I was afraid you had gone forever, never again to be together and without hope of seeing home anytime soon. Here is Takwa's gate and we're dying to get in, to face our challenge and prove this time we can win." Grace had no patience for the child or his rhymes.

"I don't understand what my eyes see; would my senses be deceiving me? Is this a trick, a challenge? Who are you strange woman, standing by my side?" The boy stared at the prince in amazement, he had not understood a word that the child had spoken; Grace had comprehended every word.

"While it might be disorienting, the scene before you is correct: you have just died and find yourself in front of a cemetery. By the way, my name is Grace." It took time for the prince to register what she had said, after which he marched straight toward the cemetery entrance.

The narrow black wrought iron gate was the only opening in the ten-foot cement and brick wall. The prince knocked three times in quick succession, using the beast headed knocker to the right side of the gate, followed by three slow thuds to the left with his fist. Grace caught up and stood not too close by his side, his ample traditional attire of double robes filled the entrance space, and the boys immediately huddled behind them. They were startled by a piercing shriek, followed by two more, seemingly out of nowhere; a putrid, dead rat smell filled the air, before them appeared an ashy-faced owl perched atop the gate.

"Who knocks at the Baron's gate?"

"I was named after my father, they called Abukari, I am known as Abukari3 because I was his third born son."

"Who are your friends?" The owl questioned. Grace answered quickly pinching the prince's side so that he let her talk.

"My name is Grace Boulay." The youngest brother squeezed his head between the two, ". . . And I'm Christo." The two other brothers might have had a chance to introduce themselves, too, only they were busy arguing who should go first. The owl had long gone before they realized their chance was wasted.

"I would prefer you learn to behave properly," the prince said to her imperiously. "I do not know who you are Grace Boulay, and based on your attire and your behavior I really don't want to know more." The prince was obviously not going to cooperate. Grace took time to observe the tall man beside her before formulating a response. His skin was the color of toasted coffee beans, it looked smooth and silky. He wore two royal robes, a long wide-sleeved white under coat, and a dark robe, singed at sides. The boots were from a fine artisan, made from supple leather, the shoe pattern perfectly cut and embroidered around the top. Grace knew he was true nobility, she had seen his kingdom.

Unbeknownst to the prince, she had mystically shared his journey and was aware of the incredible amount of knowledge he had banked behind his severe forehead. When she remembered the level of frustration she had felt upon arrival in these world-nations, Grace realized that he felt displaced, out of his element, and was struggling for some kind of control. She chose to ignore his comment.

A series of piercing shrieks cut through the night sky and the owl was with them once again; the rotting smell had lingered on awaiting his return.

"Good evening, fair prince. I have orders to let you, your lady and young friend into the Baron world-nation. You are now entering Takwa's dominion; he will be happy to take you from here and show you the way."

17

4 LEAF CLOVER NATION

"Every dog cleans itself in its own way"

A grunt then a gurgle came from behind; Grace did an about-face five feet in front of a spaghetti-looking character decked in a tight fitting, shiny, purple tuxedo jacket, tattered jeans and a black top hat. One brown eye peeped cloudily through the missing lens of his sunglasses; the other lens mirrored the startled group. He was staggering but managed to walk with a slow and deliberate swagger. His wide-open grin revealed more gaps than teeth.

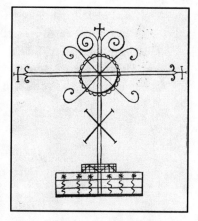

"Gade yon bèl manman bouzen!"[1] said the creature, whose name was Takwa, while leering at Grace. She had not understood what Takwa said, but Abukari3 was able to comprehend when his host spoke in tongues. He seemed to have been taken by surprise by these words, and naturally Grace wondered what the greeting had meant.

Takwa stumbled forward, closing the distance between himself and the group. Oscillating before the prince he greeted him formally by shaking hands, right to right, left to left in a cross, under and over and then over and under again three times. Abukari3's movements anticipated the ritual.

"M konnen ou gen gwo zozo pou konyen coco famn sa-a."[2] Takwa's lewd laugh led Grace to suspect that he was making embarrassing comments to the prince; she felt ashamed, self conscious and uncomfortable, disliking her host instantly.

The group walked along the dusty dirt path.

"M pral mennen nou kot papa-m, kòk li ap bande tou rèd lè l'ap wè pè tete makòmè k'ap mache avèk ou-a." [3]

Abukari3 translated for Grace: "He says he will take us to his father who will be very happy to greet us in his palace." The prince walked next to Grace and asked the boy, Chris, to remain close on the other side.

"E ti kaka sa-a, se pitit ou ?"[5]

"He wants to know who the young boy is, so I will answer that he is your cousin," Abukari3 informed Grace. She chose not to pay much attention to the conversation after that point, she didn't understand anyway. Flanked by the prince to her left and the boy to her right, Grade felt safe, Takwa swerved ahead of them. In one smooth gesture he pulled a flask from his back pocket, then wobbled a 180° turn and offered the bottle to the prince

"W'ap chofe grenn ou mon prens?"[6] Tall-dark-and-handsome took the bottle and threw back a swig, swallowed and remained expressionless; he replaced the top and handed the bottle back to Takwa.

"Tonè kraze-m gade kijan zozo-a bwè tafia piman. Nèg pa, ou gen grenn nan bounda-w!"[7]

Unaffected by this conversation, Grace began to notice the different structures they passed as they walked along the narrow path. Small stones on the dirt path cringed under her soles and the echo made her feel self-conscious; so she tried to divert her attention to her surroundings.

Baron's nation-world is the realm of the dead, and they were walking through a cemetery in his domain. It was not a typical cemetery with headstones; there was no grass, no lawn. The structures that housed the dead here contained several coffins. Some of these mausoleums looked brand new; they stood out because of fresh paint, ornate designs, and even the fresh flowers bouquets decorating the tombs. Grace noticed very few individual tombs or tombstones. These memorials were often the property of one family, and the family name was inscribed on the top. Nine to twelve individual coffin spaces were apparent from the rectangular tracings in the cement. Occupied cells usually bore the name, date of birth and death of the remnants inside; others were still empty and remained unmarked, gathering dust until the owner came to enjoy the ultimate rest along with the rest of the family. To prevent pilfering, ornate wrought iron bars and locks enclosed a few family shrines. Lucky beloved ones departed from life, often carrying these engraved thoughts with them into eternity: *Your family and friends will always love you.*

Grace thought of her own family and of the tomb built in front of the house at the beach. Maybe she was getting closer to home after all.

The group had followed the main dusty path through the cemetery thus far; then Takwa took a sudden left turn, and the group followed dutifully. Chunks of broken cement and construction materials seemed to grow out of the weeds in small, random mounds along the way. The deeper they entered Takwa's domain, the greater the space occupied by sepulchers. Rich or poor, young or old, male or female . . . everybody eventually ends up in a container, Grace found herself thinking.

Grace turned her thoughts to the beliefs she had learned in school: the body went "from ashes to ashes and dust unto dust" and the soul would face judgment before God. Here in this bizarre world-nation, a person becomes three different entities after death—the shell, gwobonanj, is that part of Cosmos which seeks isolation and aspires to join its Creator in Heaven forever; the tibonanj may wander the earth for some time, in search of its partner the gwobonanj, hoping to join it in another body for a new lifetime adventure; and the body, kadav, interred here in the cemetery, is that part of the individual that does not survive more than one lifetime whereas its partner nanm, the spirit of the essence, will wander around lost for a while

They left the secondary path and began walking between the sepulchral vaults. Here, old tombs claimed ownership of the passageway. It was uncomfortable trying to step over the long rectangular tombs. Grace felt she was desecrating or at least disrespecting the remains that were inside; so she tried her best to skirt the graves and not step on them without regard. She detected the unmistakable stench of urine, and was pretty sure she had even seen and smelled feces. But it was another smell, a rancid, putrid odor she could not place, that had her attention; it hung from the entrance at the right end of the wall where Takwa turned and entered. Steps led downwards; she held her breath and followed the group into the tomb. The dark, paved corridors lead through wall-to-wall tombs. The passage of time had erased the names of the departed from this necropolis. Even the engraved bronze plaques were illegible because of layers of melted wax that had dripped from candles.

Takwa slowed his step, which threw him off balance. He raged at the walls as though they were moving and tricking him. They reached a black iron gate blocking the entire passageway. Takwa raised his leg, planted his foot against the tomb-wall, and pulled two cigarettes out from his coat pocket. He lit both, took a drag from each, and then flipped them around, burning ends in his mouth.

"*Tonè, fout, koulangyèt manman yo; pisetig la fini!*" [8] Takwa was clearly upset because the bottle he had been nursing was empty. In a fit of rage, he smashed it on the wall and twenty-one hot peppers flew like sparklers. The noise attracted attention, causing what looked like an attendant to come to the gate.

White slacks and jacket, white shirt, and a white jasmine in the buttonhole, a rather dapper man looked nonchalantly at his watch. Quite the opposite of Takwa, this man's outfit seemed to complete his distinguished look; his deep voice commanded the respect of the group's guide, but attendant's tone seemed rather reassuring to the group. Grace couldn't understand, but she could tell there were difficulties. It seemed that the man in the Benson and Hedges get-up didn't want to let them in. The prince turned to explain:

"Our guide is negotiating our entrance. It seems that not all of us are acceptable. Don't worry: you are not the problem; I am." Grace protectively held the boy's hand.

The gate opened and only Grace and the boy entered. White-suit inspected her from head to toe and said something that she didn't understand. Then he extended his hand for a formal handshake, but when Grace's hand went to reach his, his pinky grabbed hers. She had been there, done that; so she was ready with the left pinky . . . under over, over under three times; at some point he scratched the palm of her hand with his nail. Strange, no one had done that before. She didn't know how to interpret the gesture. White-suit was apparently pleased she could follow him appropriately and he spoke to her directly. Again, she couldn't respond. He cupped his hand and caressed the boy's head, smiling and talking, but the boy couldn't understand a word either. The language barrier was so insurmountable that he finally relented and opened the gate to let in Abukari3.

Down the hall and through another gate, then they went down seven steps: first white-suit, followed by Grace, the boy, Takwa and the prince, closing ranks. At the bottom of the steps, white-suit turned 180° and faced Grace. He then proceeded to walk backwards. He motioned for her to do the same so; she turned around and also had the boy turn; Takwa knew the ritual, and Abukari3 did an about face once he reached the bottom of the stairway.

It's difficult to walk backwards, let alone in an unknown cemetery. Although they had gone down a number of sets of stairs, Grace thought she detected a sky above her. She could see the stars. Here she was, walking backwards in a cemetery in the thick of the night!

Single tombs were very rare and looked antiquated, and for this reason the white tiles of a couples' tomb attracted Grace's attention. They were set in the ground, one next the other, separated from the other tombs by a white chain affixed to four poles, arranged in a square plot. The tomb's inscription read Sergio Azzalin Canton, although Grace could barely make out the name of the other . . . Ida de Azzalin. No matter how hard she tried, Grace simply could not anticipate the rocks and other objects immediately under her step; so she cheated, peeking over shoulder and under armpit to orient herself. She thought about the couple and how their tombs joining them in death. "Till death due us part" you say when you marry; well Ida had lost her name replaced by Azzalin and was a part of this graveyard until the end of times.

They passed a structure that looked like a compound and they entered through an open gate. Walking backwards was required as they climbed the three short steps into the single story building. Grace dared not turn until specifically directed to do so. Before catching her breath, she felt a a pair of hands on her shoulders guide her to turn around; she tapped the boy ahead of her reassuringly and turned to face the unknown. To her dismay, her long-lost friend Rozalen was there, face softened by warm smile. She gave Grace a delicate peck on the cheek, all while looked at something else beyond Grace's shoulder.

"Let me see what you bring . . . Ah, Grace! You have covered quite a bit of ground since we last met; happy to see you well." She cocked her head to the side not expecting to see the boy right after Grace.

"Who's the young friend?"

Grace smiled answering mysteriously, "It's a long story."

The small room she entered was packed, forcing her to squeeze to the left with difficulty. Holding fast to Christo's hand, she struggled to follow her friend. Towards the back, it was more bearable, but just barely. Soon a strong smell of incense and a smoky fog invaded the room. A drum rumbled. Sharper tones and deeper voices joined in the percussion ensemble, preventing any kind of intelligent conversation. Three coffins filled the front of the room. After wailing and prayers and more drums and incense smoke, Grace was happy to sense the ceremony winding down and relieved when Roz nudged her to find a way to an exit.

Abukari3 was already outside, sitting under a fifty foot cotton-silk tree with a group of familiar faces. Grace noticed Angelo in the group with him and her heart skipped a beat. She remembered their past, her dream, and panicked that her vision might actually come true. Consequently, she tried to stop Rozalen from joining the crowd under the tree; but her friend was intent. When Grace noticed Anthony in the group, she knew she couldn't stop Roz's stride; so, she let her lead the way and dragged behind putting the boy before her.

Roz leaned forward and leaned her head, her arms arched in a bent line between her two opened hands, palms face down connecting with the energy of the ground:

"In the name of *Baron Samedi*, graveyard master, in the name of *Baron*

Simtye, appointed guardian of all the dead, in the name of *Baron LaCroix* home of the cross, *neg sekle kite, neg bale wouze*; three spins, three plyers, three ice picks, three hoes, *neg kokoye Meye, Neg Oloucoun.* We salute the friends of Baron and Ghede families."

18

ALWAYS STAY IN CONTROL

"Throw a rock and hide your hand."

Hatuey asked me again: "What's going on with Joel, you need to tell me everything so that I know what to do."

I explained our previous evening together at Majis' house and our escape early this morning. I quickly mentioned how this "fainting spell" had happened before. Joel expected it would happen again; that's what he had told me, we had discussed it before running into Hatuey.

"Ok, now explain to me how he got this drug in his blood, Sweetie; that's the part I don't understand."

"Have you ever heard stories about the wòch sispann?" I tried… Hatuey looked at me wide-eyed with an incredulous expression on his tanned face, sucking his teeth,

"Ah, old wives' tales, told around camp fires to spook kids! You don't really believe such a silly story? Come on! If Joel and you were messing around with something you don't want to mention that's you're business; I really don't care what you did, how you did it, or who did what. But Sleeping Beauty over there has me worried; maybe we should have taken him to a doctor. I regret coming to the island, it complicates this issue even further."

I wasn't going to be able to convince him, adding lamely, "well, the last time this happened he was out for several hours. A few times he had opened his eyes, and talked, walked and moved like he was back to normal. That's when he was the weirdest."

"Canela, my dear, you're not making sense. What were you kids doing that put a sleeping spell on our friend and a coocoo spell on you? Maybe you should get out of the sun and rest a while; why don't you come here next to me?"

He was in the shade and I was in the sun. Maybe while Joel was on his inner voyage I could rest my eyes and take a short nap; I had slept very little the night before. I left Joel's side and lay down next to Hatuey. It must have been 96 degrees in the shade, real hot so early in the morning. The salt was drying and the crystals rubbing the wrong way between the sand and my skin and made me feel itchy all over; I twitched.

Hatuey brushed the sand away from my arms and legs with his hands; his long fingers swept over me, sometimes lingering and looking for a reaction. I felt awkward and decided not to say anything; so I kept my eyes closed and faked a smile.

His touch became more precise as he took sand off, grain after grain. It tickled but then the tickle became a caress. My thoughts were jumbled; emotions and sensations were totally messing up my reasoning skills. I twitched again and inched away from him. He didn't read my body language; this, or it didn't matter because his velvet hands kept exploring the contours of my body and the feel of my skin.

I put my hand over his and held it still, saying firmly, "stop, Hatuey, I mean it! I don't want you to do that."

"Seems to me like you were enjoying it!" Hatuey's other hand started caressing my leg.

"Are you sure you want me to stop?" His left hand was now on my right thigh. Again, I stopped his hand by covering it with my own.

"What's the matter with you? Are you flipping out? I said stop and I meant it."

I got up and moved away from him. What a creep! How could I explain to Grace that Hatuey had been pawing me? This was a "lose – lose" situation if I had ever seen one.

"What's wrong, Canela? I think you're hot; we're here alone; Joel is in lala land; and Grace may never make it back from wherever she's lost. It's just you and me with this nice warm sun on your sweet skin . . . " He moved in closer to me to touch me again.

"Stop! I'm not interested."

"I love a woman who knows what she wants. I thought you were just a baby; I'm impressed, you know how to defend yourself."

What a jerk! Why was Grace wasting her time with such a loser? What could I do to get him out of my face? I ran toward the water and jumped in. The cold water splashed against me, swallowing my body; it cooled me off and allowed me to break away. Looking back at the beach, I realized Hatuey wasn't following me, so I allowed myself to enjoy the relaxing swim and began to formulate a strategy.

I was so happy I had learned how to swim; I headed straight for the deep. I wasn't afraid of the deeper water; I enjoyed it. I loved to roll forward and backwards under water, only hating when the water entered my nose. The immense sea sets me free; I feel it best when I float on my back.

I took a quick peek at the beach and saw both Joel and Hatuey outstretched on the sand and apparently resting. The timing was perfect to put my plan to action. I stayed on my back and let the current carry me away from the shore. The gentle tide pushed me to the right where, in a moment, I kicked myself past a corner of protruding rocks. I had moved out of sight of the beach. Just to make sure I hadn't been followed, I spent a few minutes in the water. This part of the beach was deserted and from the other side, neither Hatuey nor Joel was in sight. I headed for shore and looked to the sandy sea bottom like through liquid gel. I was careful for prickly sea urchins as the water got shallower and walking became easier than swimming.

A red shape in the sand attracted my attention. It looked like a piece of pottery; underwater is a strange spot for a chuck of pottery, I thought, reaching down and fishing to free it from the sand and small stones. I really enjoyed collecting shells and stones; it was a longtime hobby and I had boxes filled with all kinds "treasures." I was particularly proud of two authentic native Taino pieces of pottery.

One was round and looked like it may have been part of a pipe or other container. The other was over four inches long and half that wide, decorated with lines in set patterns and clearly seemed to have broken off a round plate. This shard looked somewhat like my two Taino pieces but was different. It was striking because of the intricate designs of small squares and lines with tiny Indian motifs sculpted in the inside. Close examination revealed multicolored shapes that made up a design whose pattern I couldn't quite make out because I only had a small part of the puzzle in my hand. Cool! A true find for my collection. I tucked it away carefully.

An uneven path of rocks lead from the beach and a path lined in candelabra cactus quickly leaded up into the hills. Funny, I hadn't remembered the island being so big. It didn't matter, I was determined to find Grace, if indeed she was here and to end this formidable adventure. After my encounter with Hatuey, I had become more worried about what had happened to my girlfriend; he acted like she wasn't going to return. Thinking back on how he explained Grace's disappearance, I became even more concerned about her safety. She had been "swallowed" by the water, he had claimed. What could make her sink to the bottom of the ocean so quickly? I wondered . . . Then

I remembered Grace not being a really a good swimmer; how would she survive in the water for such a long time? I desperately needed to find any clue that would lead to my friend.

My only clear option was to follow the path ahead. Soon voices and noises caught my ear; I could tell they were a short distance ahead, hidden by a thick growing candelabra cacti cut in a line like a fence. I heard the instruments before I saw the musicians. Three deep bellows from a bamboo trumpet gave away the nature of the band; it was a rarah.

The group was gathering at the entrance of the cacti fence that opened onto a large dirt crossroad. I noticed the caped men with shiny silk pants and then felt the sting of their whips crack through the air; the cracks sent chills down my spine, then my scalp tingled and goose bumps erupted from my head and neck down my arms and back.

The music started slowly, for it took the crowd and musicians a while before warming up; but once the bunch got into their groove, it would be one happy party all the way. I had decided to join the festivities, hoping it would lead me to Grace. After all, she had disappeared in a rarah, so maybe she would reappear because of this one. I decided no spray in the face would distract me this time. I stayed towards the back, behind the crowd. That way I had the hill to one side and people to the other. The rarah played a mix of reggae songs that paid a musical tribute to Bob Marley, a Caribbean legend.

"No woman no cry, no woman no cry,©" less a song than a collective hum, it got us going. Interrupting the gloomy tone, a soloist would punctuate the chorus after the word "cry" with a sudden "Stir it up!" to get the mood back on track. Like passing the baton in a relay race, once the crowd got tired of "No woman" another refrain would replaced it . . . "You're gonna lively up yourself.©" Although I was trying to follow the group from a distance, I had become part of the collective energy. My body reacted effortlessly to the music and I repeated the chorus like an automaton. I was light headed and my blood pulsated to the pounding drums while my frequencies tuned into the rhythmic metallic sounds made by the percussion instruments.

Soon the marching band had doubled in size, as people joined in the parade along its route. Space was tighter. While I had started toward the back right, I had moved more towards the middle-front as others joined the rarah. I had a clear spot in front of me but had to move with the flow or be trampled. I could no longer think; my emotional register had taken over. Dancing to these beats and rhythms was so familiar and natural . . . I wasn't scared or worried about anything, I felt like I had no cares in the world; my happy meter was on OK+, and it was fun to let my feet carry me.

"I wanna luv ya every day and every night©" The tune had changed yet again; so had the mood. Men got fresh and provocative, singing directly to the women in the crowd. One female voice sang out a response, it quickly caught on: "We don't need more troubles©." It became like a male/female Marley medley with the men singing, "I wanna luv ya every day and every night,©" with the women answering, "We, don't need more troubles©."

The head of the *rarah* had reached an entrance and turned left to enter. The rest of us just followed. Most were unconcerned with destination just as long as we were dancing and singing. We had entered a big yard with a magnificent silk-cotton tree. The musicians marched toward the small cinderblock house. There was no way we could all fit in that house. I guess most people thought the same because the human sea that had swept in was now ebbing away, and most people quickly disappeared back down the hill. I wanted and needed to get into the house to check it out, so I weaved my way through the remaining crowd that was slowly making its way inside.

19

SAILING THE IMMAMOU

"Bring the snake to school is one, make it sit is two."

"You look better than ever, Roz." Angelo's appreciative eyes betrayed the compliment. "But I remember you keeping better company before . . . "

Rozalen looked at Grace and Angelo, wondering why he would make such a rude comment about her friend.

"What could such a charming young lady have done to the commander of the seas to merit that insinuation?" she asked.

Anthony chuckled, amused by it all; Angelo's comment about Grace had surprised him too.

Smiling flirtatiously, Roz answered in mysterious tone, not giving Angelo a chance to answer.

"It's my pleasure to see you again Angelo, commander of the sea. If you make me some room I'll sit next to you and tell you what I've been up to lately."

He emerged from the group of men and made his way towards the spot Roz was leaving. His chocolate-cake skin looked clean and fresh.

"I'm going to have to leave you guys to all the fun; it's about time I got back on the job. With all this talk about the 'commander of the sea,' I remembered it was time I headed back to Agwe nation. The Master of the Seven Seas may need a trusted man. Anybody looking for a ride?" His question hung in the air as they all watched a cranberry colored horse with a fish tail answer his whistle and come trotting to its owner.

"Grace, weren't you going that way? Why don't you jump at this opportunity?" When she looked at the small boy, perplexed by this sudden proposition, Roz brushed away her worries.

"Ah, don't worry about Chris; I'll take care of him. We'll help him find his way." Grace's mind raced; could she really just leave for Agwe nation? She knew that the king of the sea had the power to release her from this time warp. Her only friend here was Roz, who was suggesting she go. Deep down she wanted to follow the handsome sailor; she definitely wanted to get away from Angelo. Grace looked at Abukari3 for some advice. The prince was detached, as always absent; she regretted being unable to communicate with him. She knew so much about him and his home; how could she find a way to see him again? The veve, that's how!

"So, little Miss, what will it be, will you be joining me or not?" The sailor was becoming impatient. "Few people give an island girl a break around here, I should know.

"Guess what?" Grace raised her arms, palms facing upwards. "It's all good and I'm happy and thankful to have known all of you. I know now that I will be challenged constantly, and I may or may not get a break; I am grateful and will carry that lesson with me."

Grace approached Roz, "Thank you for pointing me in the right direction. Wish me luck!" She put her arms around her friend and planted a kiss on her cheek.

"Here, I have your good luck charm," said Roz, removing two necklaces from her neck. She put one around Grace's neck and over her right shoulder and arm. She then put the second around her neck and over the other shoulder so that the necklaces formed a crisscross over her friend's chest. Grace wondered about the style but didn't have time for questions. She quickly shook Angelo's hand and skidded over to Anthony. He took her to the side and toward the back; under a Jatropha tree heavy with oily-seeds, he held a flat disk the size of a lime between her hand and both of his.

"When you wonder what to do or how to decide when faced with a difficult decision, always remember who must live with the consequences of your choices." He opened his hands showing the disc. She saw the reflection of her face in it. Anthony had given her a small mirror.

"Keep this close to you; it will help guide you through crossroads. All the answers are within you. Listen to your heart and you will find your way."

What a surprise it was to see herself again; it had been a while. Grace was happy to see that the face she remembered was the one looking back at her. Without the mirror, she saw a different person; here she looked bloated and had a funny pinkish color, like an albino seal or like upright piglet. The image in mirror reassured her; she missed her double-baked skin and was glad to see it wasn't gone forever . . . just out of current perception.

Grace rode quietly behind the man, thinking about what awaited them at the end of the journey. She would arrive in Agwe nation with a trusted member of the king's escort; that should make a good first impression, she hoped. She tried not to think ahead too much because it literally was a different world and she couldn't even guess what to expect. Her strategy was to play it smart, to develop trust needed to get permission to leave the timeless world.

Ever since their arrival in Takwa nation, the sky above was dirty grey. Although many events had taken place, the color remained unchanged neither darker nor lighter. The animal she rode moved swiftly. The mount didn't gallop; it glided. They seemed to be traveling like chalk writing on a blackboard, the ride was smooth and uneventful. It was impossible for Grace to evaluate anything here with her narrow notion of time. She knew now that that reality changes when you take away time.

Although she was quite impatient to reach their destination, Grace was relieved to feel the roan slow down and stop. They had reached a transit area were three thin, female giants waited on the icy looking surface. The tallest must have been eight feet tall, the second tallest was a head shorter and the shortest of the three was no less then six feet, six inches. Grace and her companion dismounted and went to stand on the shiny transit deck.

The shrill blast of a conch shell sounded a warning. Then the platform they were standing upon began to sink into the ground. It was like being inside a Swiss cheese. Tunnels opened up before them with passageways of different sizes leading to various destinations. The giants entered a tunnel and faded away.

"I hope you enjoy traveling on water; it's my favorite way home." He had finally talked to her. Grace wanted to make conversation and needed to gather some information; so she began with a pleasant rejoinder.

"Which ever way is best for you is great by me." She tried to keep him talking. "So why is water travel your favorite?"

"Every time I chose to travel by boat," he replied calmly, "I pray for the souls of my people who sailed over many seas, and I ask that all their descendants walk in the light." The answer was spontaneous and spoken serenely but with passion; the words went straight to Grace's heart.

"Who are your people?" Her question took him aback.

"My story starts with the ancient ones, the first to walk upright; they traveled by land, then over ice and conquered water. After that, mankind spread around the earth and to all lands. Truly, they are all my people. But from those roots have sprung many blossoms giving birth to well-known civilizations, and these are my blood, too: the Mandingo, Egyptians, Nubians, Dahomeans, Congolese, Ethiopians, and Berbers—all people of color worldwide felt their influences."

Grace and her companion had entered a short tunnel of light that took them to a dock where a steamboat waited. He continued talking as the two of them boarded along with the animal.

"Tell me," he said in a friendlier tone, "what do you know about the history of your people? I'd like to know where they were from and how they traveled to the place where you were born."

"I too come from the First to walk upright, and I was told that my hair is the crown they left me for inheritance. My peppercorn tiara could also celebrate royal blood that I would have inherited from the Arawak Indians. I don't really know much more about my ancestors, though. What I have told you comes from my parents and information I gathered here." Grace continued,

"In school I learned that the Taino and Arawak were the native populations that Columbus found on my Caribbean island. Less than one hundred years later they had all died of mistreatment and diseases that arrived with the discoverers. Slaves came from Africa because the Europeans needed free labor in the New World. My parents told me about their parents and a family tree, that's why I know that my dad's family line started on this island with a freed slave named Bonnie. My mom's family tree is the one with Indian blood."

"I guess conversations about ancestors and bloodlines aren't very interesting to you, too far removed from your daily life."

"Actually, I enjoy hearing old stories about my parents, grandparents and their parents. Often, I come off as too emotional to some of my friends when I talk about the genocide of the Indians, or slavery or our battles for independence. Some people tell me that these things happened hundreds of years ago and that I take them too personally. How can I not be emotional about my history? It determined who I am today. It's painful to think of a past of shackles, abuse, and humiliation; how do you flip it around to create success?"

"'Enough already!'" others say; "'it's been over eight generations.' Well, maybe being a slave changed my ancestors DNA . . . I sometimes feel I inherited a boiling rage hard to control in the face of injustice. I actually think that because my ancestors had to swallow titanic doses of anger and resentment it became second nature, and having nowhere better to go it reprogrammed their systems. I will admit to you that aggressiveness sometimes bursts out of me and I don't know where it comes from, certainly not from my experiences in this lifetime."

The serious man had not expected to hear such passionate words. He let his eyes drift along the images of a place he knew by heart. Agwe nation was bustling with activity; traffic and people were everywhere. Built above ground, its unforgettable skyline consisted of bridges and geometrically shaped structures that connected in the air. The cement jungle trapeze was home to a dense population.

Grace and her companion were arriving. The sky was tinted with hues of tangerine and pink and the port air smelled of piña colada and banana bread.

"Where do your traveling plans take you in this busy city of mine?"

Not knowing what to expect of this new level, Grace was unprepared for the scene coming to life before her eyes. She hadn't the foggiest idea where or how she was going to see the head of this nation-world to ask permission to return home. She took her own sweet time before answering.

"I don't know what I was expecting, but certainly not this," she said, motioning toward the city before her. "It changes my perception of how I will deal with this realm."

The man towered over her. She raised her gaze to meet the dark of his eyes, just long enough for her to fear the immensity of a black hole.

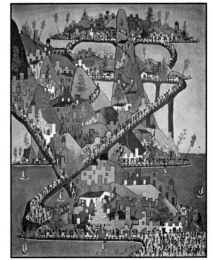

"My purpose here was to find the door that exits this plane and enters onto mine. I hoped to be allowed through, the quicker the better. This trip with you, though, has changed my pace; I would like to learn about this wonderful place. If your obligations will allow, maybe you could share some of your world with me."

Her honesty pleased him and the tone of her request stroked his ego. This being wasn't made of wood; Grace was rather persuasive. His smile revealed a boyish shyness, although his baldhead and ageless skin made it impossible to pinpoint his age.

"Well, I work, so that limits my availability. If you don't mind just hanging around while I tend to my responsibilities, it will be my pleasure to show you around town afterwards."

As it happened, Agwe's palace was the first stop. Set in the middle of a small island connected to the mainland with two arched bridges, it was the heart of the city and of its people. In the center stood a conch shell palace with neither doors nor windows; dried algae partitions tinkled softly with the wind.

Grace waited a long while at the entrance. After boredom had chased her best resolutions away, she wandered around to see what, if anything, she could find. Her feet strolled along white pebble paths that led to benches placed for visitors to rest; fountains spurted water in harmonious designs creating fluid sculptures. Sea grape trees were everywhere; taller and older trees weighed under the heavy packs of green grapes; the thick, waxy, oval leaves stretched over yellow veins and looked like plastic. She moved closer and verified that they were like back home; the texture felt natural not plastic at all.

Beyond the tree, she noticed a pond. It brought back the memory of Lasiren and Labalenn and she decided to follow a path in another direction. Her attention went toward a rock formation that hung over what looked like the entrance to a cave.

The short walk allowed her to inspect a nine-foot boulder. From afar, she thought it depicted a turtle; closer inspection revealed the crudely carved traits of a human face with thick lips, a broad nose, and heavy brows. Grace found it hard to resist curiosity and entered the cave.

In the first chamber, there was a pool; she marveled at the sunlight peeking through a small opening and shining through the transparent water from the top. She should have seen it coming, but did not expect the curious menagerie splashing and relaxing in the sinkhole. Lasiren's body was two-thirds under water; her tail rested affectionately on a fifteen foot blue and white whale.

"So you've made it all the way to my husband's palace? Congratulations Grace . . . Will you take the time to greet him, talk, and then leave? Or will this be your usual, wham, bam, I'm out of this jam?"

Lasiren embarrassed Grace, who didn't like having her weaknesses aired in front of strangers. Though, in all honesty, she had exited the Legba, Lasiren and Labalen nations rather inelegantly. She had to make sure to win Agwe to her side; he was the powerful master of the seven seas. Ayizan, though, was her ally and she had hopped, skipped, and glided out of Takwa with no major friction. With Agwe on her side, she had a powerful protector. Antagonizing Lasiren further would not fix her situation, so she let the Mystery's comment slide.

"Hello everybody. How good to see you Lasiren!" she said, wearing a confident smile.

"Please, call me *Nayilé*, the name I go by in Agwe nation."

"Nayilé it is." Grace was uneasy, unsure what to say, and did not know how to leave graciously; but she wasn't going to let it show. Fruit and flower trees filled the area; she recognized the tall mango, tamarind, and breadfruit trees, and the shorter cherry and guava trees studded about, colorful hibiscus bushes and white camellia flowers claimed most of the remaining space.

The array of animals around Nayilé was bizarre; the tallest of the group were the two giraffes chomping on leaves ten feet away. Grace moved in closer and noticed two tigers in a tree across from the giraffes; another mermaid, this one small and honey colored sat on the lowest branch of the same silk-cotton tree as the black striped yellow tigers.

"Why don't you join us? I'll introduce you to my friends," Nayilé offered. A bit apprehensive, Grace took up the challenge. She entered the water knee deep before laying eyes on a seal that looked like a small lioness; it lay right in front of Nayilé's whale. Nipping playfully at the seal/lion's tail under water was another whale. Flat on its back, a masculine looking shorthaired, brown skinned mermaid backstroked across the water. A frisky silver swordfish jumped out of the water into the air and dove back into the water with a splash.

"You must be forewarned," noted Nayilé, "once you dip in the pool of clarity, from then on you will see things for what they are." Something tickled Grace's knee. She looked down to find a rainbow trout as long as her leg turning circles and swishing its tail making bubbles.

"I would think it would be an advantage to see things clearly," Grace responded.

"Don't be so sure," Nayilé interrupted, "It's often more convenient to ignore the plain truth. Where are my manners? I haven't presented anybody yet. "Anacaona," she called to the golden mermaid, "and Caonabo," motioning to the water, "this is Grace." Both barely nodded their head in recognizance.

"Tell me, how did you get through the palace gates?"

"Well, I got a ride in Takwa nation and was lucky enough that it was coming right here."

"Who could have been coming from Takwa and would give you a ride here?" Grace didn't have the answer to that question, for she had not caught the name of the attractive man with whom she traveled. She avoided answering the question directly.

"Nayile, did I hear you say that your friends names were Anacaona and Caonabo? Just like the most famous Taino queen and king who resisted the Spaniards but who, in the end, were captured and murdered?"

"So you do know some of your history. Yes, you are correct; Earth has always had its share of beings of light as well as those of darkness. Their passage in your world and in the time you refer to was their last. They are the same, for energy cannot be lost, nor destroyed and their life force has transformed. Caonabo was a prisoner traveling to Spain when his captors thought he had died onboard. As was the custom, they tossed his human remains overboard; but his noble soul had not perished at sea. What happened was that he channeled the spirit of Baron, he looked and smelled dead, the well-known traits displayed by people mounted by Baron's spirits. Therefore, once his jailors tossed him overboard, my husband immediately sent for him and prepared his arrival royally, as he well deserved. He has remained a favored guest in Agwe nation ever since.

During your visit in my world, you thought I had no friends, which is why you acted so arrogantly. In fact, I have many wonderful friends and various palaces and I travel as I please."

With the newfound wisdom gently seeping in, Grace understood Nayilé's words, measuring the weight of her actions since their last encounter. She had been deluding herself, for her strategy to escape and run ahead was destructive. What she wanted most was out of this reality; but she wasn't going about it the right way . . . At least she knew what she wanted, so her goal was clear.

The process of going through this world was the important part, but she was rushing it. She was missing the point and if she missed the point she would not be able to leave. Grace clearly understood she needed to get her act together. She was in Agwe nation now, so she had to make the most of an opportunity to see Agwe. She had to take a shot at reaching her goal, even if she had flubbed each step so far. Then again, she had made it here, so she must have done something right.

"Nayile, how do I prepare to see Agwe? Will you tell me that, please?"

Lasiren smiled. "I see that you have learned to be less arrogant—one lesson learned since we last met. In order for you to meet my husband, I would recommend you offer him a service. Let me describe a traditional service to Agwe. Certain things are essential: you will need a conch shell, a bottle of champagne, anisette, white wine, and coffee with both sugar and cream. He likes cane syrup, melons, boiled cornmeal, rice cooked in coconut milk, fried ripe bananas, cake, white roosters, white ram goats, and ducks. The gifts he favors are perfumes, mirrors, nautical medals, fishhooks, model boats, and rowing oars. You must not forget a white candle."

"Find a clear spot to set your service," Nayilé advised. "Then cover your altar with a blue cloth and place a big wine goblet of water in the center. On the back of the table or pinned to the wall, or skirt of the tablecloth, put an image of St. Ulrich."

"You must dress in blue, any shade of blue you like; and tie your head with a blue or white scarf. Set up pictures of the sea with boats, and your seashells and conch shell. Then lay out the food and other offerings."

"Finally, light your candle, and pray the Our Father, the Hail Mary, and the Apostle's Creed. Then, you will call Agwe, by blowing into the conch shell so that Agwe can join you in your service. You will say:

Met Agwe! Met Agwe Tawoyo, Koki Lame. Come here for your service! Captain of the Seven Seas, husband of Lasiren, eternal Sailor, and Seaman!"

"Set your white candle in the center of the altar, and present the gifts you have for Agwe to the four corners: North, South, East and West. Offer Agwe all the gifts you have for him. Then dance for Agwe while singing this song:

♫*Anonse, Ozany nan dlo Oba Kosou Miwa, Lawe-Lawe! anonse... Ozan·y nan dlo... Oba Kosou Miwa, Lawe-Lawe! nan Lavil Okan e.... kriòl mande shanjman!* ♪"

"After you are finished, ask for that which you desire Met Agwe to do for you. Remind him, that you have just conducted a beautiful service for him and that now it is his turn to do you a favor. Leave the area and allow the candles to burn out. Then dispose of all the food offerings in the sea, where Met Agwe can come and take them away."

What a complicated program! Wow! Grace was surprised she had so many things to do, and no clue where to find all the ingredients Nayilé had enumerated. Where to start? All of this to arrange a meeting with Agwe! She thought of asking Nayilé for more help and then decided against the idea; the Lwa had given her ample information and the time had come for her to be more self-reliant.

"I would like to have a word with the Golden Flower Queen, if I may."

"Please do, why don't you join her under the tree."

Although not a mermaid, Grace quickly swam the distance that separated her from Anacaona. The queen's head seemed to irradiate sunlight.

"I have come to pay my respects to you, Queen of the Cariban people. I am a child of your line from the land that was your own."

The call of her beloved Kiskeya found resonance in the beautiful queen. Since the genocide of her people, rarely did she speak; the pain had sealed her lips and muted her voice. Anacaona looked at Grace and recognized the natural elegance and look of class she saw in her beloved Caonabo before his capture. Something about the young lady was kindred to her people. . . The ancient ones had foretold of this time, she was remembering now.

Beings of light would walk upright as they had before, some of them with the memories of the native civilizations of the New World. But these beings would also be prepared for the times ahead when Earth would move into its next dimension. She felt the acceleration of time and almost felt joy; finally, the World will reach a higher frequency, making it possible to move onto the next plane, so that man delights in a time of higher knowledge, and humanity can continue its cycle of evolution.

"Woman of my blood line, daughter from my homeland, you seem familiar yet totally foreign to me. I should have known this time was soon to come because of the ancient prophecies. Wise ancestors such as the Maya had knowledge of cycles of the constellations and planets in our galaxy and they charted these movements, seeing the cosmic past and predicting the future of their own planet. They provided future generations with astrological calendars to help them understand the upcoming planetary events. You are from the children of the *mestizos* and will be going back to our homeland. Please tell them to keep the traditions; children need to learn the stories of the past to situate them in the present and to make way for what the future has in store. Not the revisionist's history, created to bring shame on all races, but the real story of humankind and its adventure on Earth."

Grace felt goose bumps all over her skin.

"Because life on Earth is bound by flesh, man struggles to control time; yet, time is an illusion. Deepen your discernment of all energy that surrounds you, regardless of its source. Seek answers about the mother of creation, called Isis by the Egyptians, and the time when the Milky Way aligns with the center of the universe."

Grace remained silent and motionless waiting for the Queen to finish. Her voice had returned, touching upon a new frequency that sounded to Grace like the metallic ring of a triangle; she heard it through her ears, and it activated the area of her third eye . . . She felt Anoli tickling her hand!

"Soon will be the World of the Fifth Sun, this era will start when Earth aligns itself with the center of the galaxy and the solar meridian crosses the galactic equator. On this day, the sun crosses the intersection of the Milky Way and the ecliptic plane. These events signal the embodiment of the Sacred Tree of Life, and will open new channels for cosmic energy to flow to Earth, cleansing it and all that dwells upon it, rising all to a higher level of vibration. Look, there is a bag hanging on the trunk of this tree; take it, it contains three ears of corn. You will plant this corn on my land to prepare for my return after the fulfillment of the prophecies. "

Grace remained hypnotized by the message for a while. When she regained her senses, she promised Anacaona to tell people about the upcoming World of the Fifth Sun so that those willing can prepare and be ready. She thanked the queen for her words. Unusually emotional, she now wanted to leave this area and quickly made her way to the shore. Although she tried to take leave of Nayilé, the Gatekeeper detained her.

"I want to give you a gift before you go . . . Here," she said, handing Grace her comb, "take this and use it to comb your hair." Grace took the gift and approached Nayilé respectfully; she brushed her lips against the Gatekeeper's hand.

"Goodbye Mistress of the Sea. I will remember you. Thank you for the lovely gift; I will cherish it, as I will cherish our special friendship."

She hurried out of the cave and bumped into her friend on his way in.

"I've been looking for you everywhere!"

Grace was startled by the run-in and was also flustered by her encounter in the pool of wisdom.

"Sorry, I got lost and couldn't find my way." After a few deep breaths, she regained her composure.

"Thanks for coming for me; I couldn't ask for help, I didn't even know your name to justify how I got in here in the first place!"

"I'm called Balendjo, authentic Batioke Nago. I originated in Three Islands, and I'm an original Oloukoun also known as Negblabla."

"Well, that's a mouthful, I don't have quite as many names, you can just call me Grace; and, may I call you Negblabla?" His smile was her only answer.

"Let's go, I'm going to give you a short tour of the outer kingdom. Later, I have to return here. Our first stop will be the market; it's the most colorful and complete of any other world/nations, and the place to get anything you need. "

20

Heart Pierced Danto

"Even in hell there are favorites."

Standing room only, the space was too small for this many people. I felt cramped and uncomfortable. Strangers invaded my personal space and their strong smells gagged me. I really hated the musky odors penetrating through my skin and nose. I was drawn to six musicians banging on drums that bellowed big booms inside my rib cage; the echoes made by metal clings guided my steps. I felt the maracas' repetitive swish and clash hypnotize my attention; as if on automatic pilot, I rapidly adjusted to my surroundings.

I was outside of my normal control zone once I had walked through the door, but I just *had* to find out what was in here. Breathing deeply and focusing my awareness enabled me to remain conscious and register the events taking place around me. I tried to move toward the music slowly, inconspicuously, and dared not take in too much too quickly.

The middle-pole caught my attention first and from there I figured it out; it hung from the ceiling in the middle of the room but didn't reach the floor. Like a sunbeam radiating from the center, the ritual departed from the middle of the room and moved outward. Immersed in the rumbling drums I could only see part of the ceremony, but couldn't make out the full picture, so I pushed forward.

Finally, I reached the front row and could move ahead no more, unless I joined the dancers. Over seventy-five people danced before me, mostly women with colorful scarves around their heads. Dag! I didn't have a scarf and I couldn't dance like them; so I had come to a standstill.

This was my reason talking; I could hear it loud and clear in my head. The vibrations of the music drowned out the voice of talking reason, though; they came in through my ears, but also seemingly through my pores I was drinking in the music, encountering oscillations I had been craving at the core. It made me feel different, like another part of me had taken command over my body.

I noticed my body moving, enjoying the beat and relishing this rhythm. I was feeling good all over. I let it flow and could sense the gestures amplifying my connection with the sounds. I looked around and imitated other people; they each had their own style but were basically dancing the same step. If I had another purpose for being there it had been long forgotten.

"Curly-head rasta! I knew I would see you here." I felt a shove on my shoulder but paid it no mind.

"Oooo, girl, you're gone! My, I got here just in time; you need to get ready *now*."

I didn't have a chance to react, nor did I have the time. The friendly stranger tied a deep blue satin scarf around my head and spun me around by the shoulders. When we faced each other, I recognized the woman from the wosh sispan; she handed me another red scarf folded in a triangle. I tied a knot at the narrow ends around my hips.

My friend then took my hand and coached me to dance—just what I had been looking for. Soon I knew what to do and was ready for the next step. We moved closer to the middle-pole.

♫ *Sèt kout kouto, sèt kout ponya, prete m basen an, pou m vomi san mwen* ♪

An Indian-looking person in front of me jumped out of her skin. Her Madonna-shaped face took on a distressed look; long thick braids bounced off her shoulders, shaken by spasms. The crowd around me opened from the middle to let a man through. He held a candle in one hand and in the other, pale-yellow maracas trapped in a net of colorful beads. Hypnotized by the maracas, I gazed as the celebrant shook the startled lady's hand, crisscrossing right to right, and left to left; then flipping over and under and then under and over and again. After which they started talking almost casually and he handed her a lit cigarette. One of the people dressed all in white sprinkled her with perfume from the long neck of a silver-foil covered bottle; she loved it, and a lightly florid scent of cologne filled the room. Then they went around talking to people, the celebrant guided her around the room, and then back towards the middle; all the while, drumbeats pounded.

The push of the crowd jolted me out of my reverie. I recognized Toussaint walking toward the middle pole with a small black goat wrapped around his shoulders. With his arms stretched forward, he presented the animal to the four corners, then to the celebrant. Then he tied it to a stump. The celebrant, his initiates and the woman converged around Toussaint, who presented the animal to them. She stood the goat on its four legs, knelt down close and tied a shiny red scarf around its neck. She seemed to whisper softly into its ear, and she settled the animal with the gentle stroke of her hand.

"Who's the Indian?" I asked my newfound friend.

"Poopeet comes from a village not too far away where descendents of the native Taino Indian population remain. She is also a member of this community, a *pitit lakou*, because our community and religious leader, Ganngan, cured her with his traditional medicines."

Poopeet's puffy lids distracted from her captivating eyes.

"Words I will speak come from days buried far away; the messages I deliver today were sent by the initiators: the first who walked and claimed this land. These people believed in Deminem Caracol and Yayayel; they respected Earth and worked together to feed all children."

Holding the goat by its four legs, she draped the animal around her shoulders and swayed to the drumbeat, pausing at the North, South, East, and West.

♫ *La fanmi san m yo, gen yon jou ya bezwen mwen, ya chache mwen mesye, le yo we mwen yo kwe m se vakabon, yo kwe m se sanzave, yon jou yo ka bezwen mwen mesye* ♪

Then, she sat the goat on a cement bench to the side of the room; a cement block propped up the animal's body and its four legs hung to the side not quite reaching the ground. Toussaint took a skinny knife with a wooden handle from the heart shaped figure traced under the middle-pole and handed it to her. Poopeet slowly turned the animal's head to face her, exposing the area where she was going to strike.

I was afraid to look. Was she really going to slit the defenseless animal's throat? Poopeet's two black braids fell to each side of her narrow hips, With a solemn expression, she lifted her head and arms up in adoration and brought her hands down to her chest in prayer and respect. I watched the shinny metal drop and the worn brown handle hit the ground blending-in immediately with the brown dirt floor.

"No more blood!" she incanted.

Poopeet looked around the room.

"No blood from this animal will be shed. It will live to multiply; the offering will be in celebration of life. Blood sacrifice must from now on be symbolic; the significance is the preservation of the lifeline, to provide future generations with the traits they'll need. The chosen animals ears will be pierced and they will be left to graze free, their lives dedicated to the angels."

Other participants had possessions like the Indian woman, and each time they would follow the ritual with perfume; they all smoked cigarettes and sometimes would take a swig of rum. The music changed and so did the spirits. An initiate draped in a red cape was smoking a cigar. Presented with a machete he deftly slung it by his side.

♫ *Balendjo oh oh se pa manje ranje ki pou touye chwal Banlendjo*♪

I observed the new behavior, intrigued. Total shock! He walked straight up to me. He spoke in tongues that I was unable to understand. The celebrant came to my rescue.

"You can settle your heart; your friend is fine. Very soon you will be together, all the requirements are fulfilled. Be aware, when you see her she will no longer look at the world as you do: through your navel. Yes, I know you"! No need to look at me with that puzzled look. Over half of the world is constantly suffering; children do not have enough food to eat, yet you feel no shame, no discomfort, though you are surrounded by too many things you don't need a live in a world where so much goes to waste. As long as your belly is full and your wishes fulfilled, you give no thought to the other half of the World. Grace will come back changed. She has reached a higher level of understanding; she senses her connection to the whole and knows the individual part she must play. She will be looking from the outside of the cosmos into her world and from there into her own space, quite a different perspective."

I didn't really understand the full meaning of his words, but I knew it was important. I hung on to the first thought: Grace was going to be okay, and we would be together soon . . . cool, real cool! The rest, well maybe he was right; I did spend a lot of time and energy worrying about lil 'ol me.

He left me to my thoughts and to my friend.

She looked at me with a smile. "Ready for some fresh air now? Let's go for a walk."

It was time to go; although I wasn't sure where else we could go.

Negblabla had selected a secluded bay at the bottom of the hill where the arches met on Agwe's island. Nearby, a clear stream trickled through pebbles, silt and sand and disappeared into the sea. On an elevated round sandstone with a flat top Grace set an altar with a blue table cloth. She made the sides drop evenly and thought about her visit to the heart of the city riding behind Negblabla on Gwojoel, the marine horse. Negblabla had a special way with words; maybe that's why they called him blabla, even if he was a man of few words. Her companion felt a fantastic sense of belonging and responsibility toward Agwe nation; these feelings inspired Grace; he kindled her sense of community with her own home. Negblabla also had a way of making her face her responsibilities, being so serious and responsible himself. In fact, he made her feel unique, special, and seemed to show a sincere appreciation for whom she was and what she thought. Grace really liked the maturity he expected from her; he brought out the woman in her, although she was still a young lady.

She set the champagne bottle, conch shell and fish hook on the altar. She also had some food: white rice cooked with coconut milk, fried ripe plantain, and hadn't forget the cake, or coffee and cream. She tied her head with the aqua green scarf that an Indian-looking lady with braids hanging down to her waist had offered her. Finally, she lit the white candle.

First, she presented the offerings to the four cardinal points. Next, she sat Indian style, facing the ocean. Grace focused on inner silence and controlled her breathing; then, she said the Our Father and a short spontaneous prayer asking for guidance. She felt a warm breeze brush against her cheek and she opened her eyes.

How long had he been there she didn't know; she hadn't heard a thing. She had not begun the call to Agwe, who could this man be in front of her? They observed each other in silence for a while.

"Staring at me, you wonder who I am; yet you have prepared a service for me. Do you not know me?"

Could this be Agwe? Sure, she had prepared a service, but she certainly hadn't expected him to show so fast! Quick as a wink, Agwe had startled Grace, but she didn't loose her wits.

"Papa Agwe, ruler of the Seven Seas, I have prepared this service for you." Before she could continue, he had begun to talk.

"Yes, mhmm, this is nice, very nice, thank you, really. But this approach, like me, is getting old!"

Grace admired his full head of curly white hair that he wore like a cloud-crown. His magnetic green eyes spoke of the sea, as did the indeterminate layers of tans simmered into his sunny skin. He was a stunningly good-looking man; you could say he looked like a movie star.

"I'm expecting more from you. You are from the modern times when man has the weapons to destroy the entire planet and more. Tell me now if I got it right: you know how to end the world but you still haven't figured out why it was created or what your individual contributions mean, right?"

How the world was created or evolved—this depends on whose version you accepted, although Grace wasn't sure why. As for individual responsibility—lots of people didn't bother to ask such questions; others had their own opinions and beliefs; and some think that their answer is the best. What did the sum of this mean to the cosmos? She didn't have a clue. Agwe was right.

"You're right; that's us." Agwe flashed a smile that twinkled like a string of pearls.

"Remember that what you learn through human emotion becomes a part of you forever. During your human life it's important to accumulate energy from emotional experiences; the type of emotion is crucial when you consider the baggage you will carry along."

"Master of the Seas, how could I take that message back with me and deliver it for all to hear?" Agwe was surprised and a bit confounded. Creasing his forehead, the long curls of his eyebrows touched in the middle.

"So you want to leave us already? Didn't you just get here? Wasn't this your first service to me? Why the rush? You sure are from the modern generation!

How quickly you have understood *all* there is to learn. And now you're ready to move on! Or, rather, you just want to return to the comfort of your life."

Grace did want to go back home. She was pouring so much energy into reaching that goal that she really wasn't consciously tuned into anything else. She had just recently realized she had been rushing. In all honesty, she hadn't given much thought to lessons learned here. Because of Anoli and the veve, she had been able to displace and join Abukari3 on his learning adventure. That voyage into the world's collective experience enabled her to accumulate a vast array of information on nature, the environment, plants, their properties and preparations, and so much more. Why remember all that stuff anyway, why would that be helpful? Back home she would go to the doctor who provided the prescriptions for medicine.

"Master Agwe, don't our worlds communicate, isn't there a way the keepers of world nations transmit their vibrations and messages to Earth?"

Agwe enjoyed the cake but complained the coffee was cold. He thanked her nonetheless with a larimar stone ring, which she promptly slipped on her middle finger.

"I see you do have many things figured out if you understand that communication happens on many levels. However, you have yet to fully appreciate your situation if you finally return home."

"There is no way for you to return to yourself and your life back home. You are changed and you will realize this more each day. Trust that the lessons you have learned here will help you face the new reality you will find after you leave. Many like you have experienced different dimensions. What happens with the knowledge? How you apply your special talents will be the measure of your success. Your harmonic balance will indicate the energy you accumulated and will allow or deny your preparedness for the next level. Your cellular memory may have propelled you to face your destiny, but only you can determine exactly how to fulfill your zetwal. What will happen when history knocks at your door? Will you be ready? How have you prepared your answer?"

Grace didn't know what to answer; destiny hadn't been an issue in her life so far. People with destinies were people who were born to be famous. They had amazing talents that projected them into the spotlight. Grace had never experienced anything extraordinary before this life changing adventure.

"Finally at a loss for words, dear?" Agwe's asked, a bit sarcastically.

"Well now, why don't you take some time to mull over what you want to answer and then think carefully about what you will ask of me during your next service. You know what they say? 'Be careful what you pray for because you just might get it.' Meanwhile I need some ingredients to prepare medicine for my good friend Zili. Take your time to think while you fetch me the things on this list."

"Yes, sir." Arrogant Grace had been humbled to monosyllabic answers.

Good thing she knew her way to the market. Agwe nation's modern inner city was relatively small and Grace went over the list while she walked the short distance:

9 sweet basil leaves
¾-pound marine algae
3 white candles
21 anise stars

She was still wearing the scarf the lady with the two braids had given her. Her benefactor smiled as she saw Grace approach the stand.

"I like the scarf on you; tell me, luv, did you come to get another?"

Grace touched her head. "Your gift brought me good luck, and I came to thank you."

The dark copper toned woman's oil eyes shined. "Your prayers were answered?" she inquired.

Grace thought before answering. "Let's say, I'm moving closer to going home."

The lady tilted her ratty sombrero backwards, "If what you want is to leave I have your solution. You must bring back three leaves of basil when they ask you for nine; if you are to find some marine algae make sure to return with grass instead. Think about it . . . Too good a servant becomes invaluable; masters will want to keep your services forever. That's what I know." There was good logic to what the lady had said.

Grace meandered through the marketplace, picking up the items she needed and thinking about the Indian lady's advice. Where she came from, getting things right was prized. Would Agwe be angry because of her stupidity? His tantrums were legendary; there was no knowing how he could react. On the other hand, maybe to get out of this world-nation being right wasn't as important as getting results. If her release to go home was the result, she was more than willing to follow the lady's advice. Decisions, decisions . . .

What was likely to happen when she got home? She wondered if she would find her family right away. How much time had gone by on Earth since she crossed over into world-nations? How about if they were no longer in Port Salut and they had left and gone home? How about if they thought she was dead and already had her funeral! Nah! She thought they wouldn't give up on her without finding her body. How about this bloated body? Would she look like herself back home? Or was her body altered forever by this adventure? Would people accept her explanations? She doubted it; she could not imagine this experience before and had been reticent throughout. Grace wondered what she would do and say. She took out Anthony's gift mirror to look at who would have to live with the consequences of her decision.

The thump of hooves on the ground attracted her attention. How lucky! Negblabla was coming her way and she could ask him about the lady's advice; could this be a coincidence? Gwojowel came to a halt in front of her; she patted his head playfully and flattered his thick neck greeting him with a soft voice.

"Funny Earth person! She greets my animal before me."

"Hello," Grace mumbled, feeling her face flush and her heart racing; she tried to hide the effect he had on her. She was surprised the joy she felt seeing him again.

"Coming from the market?"

"Yes, in fact I'd like to talk to you about the market, if it's not inconvenient."

Negblabla knew the lady, so it made it easier to update the story since the gift of the scarf; Grace explained their more recent conversation.

"You know, Grace, you were born with a zetwal, your destiny for your time on Earth. You must know that only you can determine how you will face your life situations and you will determine their outcomes; your attitude counts, as well as your actions or lack of; your choices reveal the keys that open the passageway to accomplishments and failures. How you react and learn from your experiences and mistakes must be of your free will. I'm sorry, but I can't advise you what to do. It's too important that you face this one alone; I've got your back though; I'll be around for you whatever you choose to do." He put his hand inside his vest and out came a maraca, the kind made from a gourd and covered by a mesh net of colored glass beads. "Tchsh tchsh tchsh," the maracas sounded their abrasive vibration.

"Here, take this, it's a gift."

"Thanks!" Grace tried out the instrument . . . "Tchsh, tchsh."

"That's the sound you'll make when you would like to contact me. It's going to take some practice, but that maraca is tuned to my frequency, and I will feel the vibrations wherever I am."

There was not much more to say between them but neither seemed inclined to leave. The conversation continued about the visit they had earlier and they talked about each place they had visited in detail. Neither wanted to leave, sensing it was probably the last time they would be seeing each other in this place. Negblabla finally offered to take her back to Agwe palace but Grace preferred to walk and have time to think.

"I must admit, this was far less unpleasant than I anticipated. I wouldn't mind seeing you again sometime." His warm smile betrayed the joke and she understood he was teasing her.

"Well, I didn't mind spending time with you either; maybe you can pay me a visit if you're on the Earth plane some day." She managed some humor of her own, but didn't expect him to answer so quickly,

"I think I can arrange that, I'll let you know when I'm in your neck of the woods."

What else was there left for her in these world-nations? She walked on the dirt path to the conch palace, listening to the pennants whistling in the wind, She took the sweet basil out and smelled the pungent dark green leaves, then arranged all the ingredients in the packet she collected for Agwe. She ran into a palace servant before reaching the entrance.

"Agwe has been impatiently waiting for this; it wasn't wise for you to take so much time to return. He isn't in the best of moods. Hopefully you got it all right!" Grace trembled as she handed the packet.

"You are to wait in the courtyard for the results."

She strolled into a park laid in black and white pebbles, and sat down on a bench next to a cement flowerpot the size of a fire hydrant. It reminded her of Canela and a story she had told her about breaking her leg with a big cement pot when she was a child.

"FOUT TONERRE!" Grace froze when she heard the scream. "Thunder and lightning! Blasted! Get rid of her! DAMN IT! Send her away I say; tell her to go and never come back! Take her to the orange tree and make sure she leaves! ADIEU!"

A hopeful smile curled the side of her mouth, but her heart thumped hard enough to make her eyelashes flutter; she tried to breathe short breaths, waiting for the servant's response. Bursting with impatience, she ran towards the palace as the servant came rushing out and motioned to Grace.

"Come, you must hurry; he's furious. Quickly come this way to the orchard." Rows of orange trees planted in reddish brown dirt extended further than Grace could see. The servant walked without hesitation down three rows and across to the seventh tree.

"Did you climb trees when you were a child?" Although athletic, Grace had never been a tomboy and her mother wouldn't have allowed her little girl to climb trees.

"I don't think so," she replied not amused.

"Well, you're going to have to learn now if you want to leave and go home. Here take this pouch. Inside are pearls; you will give one to each person you tell this story."

Grace fondled the precious stones before placing the pouch in the bag with Anacaona's corn. She didn't think about her options very long. She just concentrated upon breathing deeply, calling Anoli to her hand before placing it, as usual, on her shoulder.

Branching out from the bottom, the tree was easy to climb. She was able to put her foot on low branches and move up gradually. There were thorns though, big green thorns on the trunk and small branches, so she had to be careful. Anoli jumped from her shoulder onto a branch ahead of her.

"There you go, buddy, show me the way." Grace waved the servant goodbye and followed the lizard up and out the top of the tree. Anoli made its way to the very last branch and waited for Grace. At this level, her body was still under water but her head and neck were above and she gazed around at what looked like land.

Grace put her head into the water to call the critter to stay with her, but it had started on its way back down. She hesitated, wanting to go after her new little friend, and then understood that Anoli wasn't from Earth world but of other world-nations. It had chosen to return were it belonged.

EPILOGUE

"You ask yourself the meaning of the ritual you just saw and are probably wondering why your friend was there," observed my acquaintance, whose name I didn't know. "I could read your reaction and your expressions of disgust anticipating the sacrifice."

She was right; I thought I was going to pass out in there. As for Toussaint, well . . .

"There is a reasonable explanation, you know? You could say there is the Old World way and there is the New World way; just as there is the Old Testament and the New Testament, same God, but different times require different rituals."

"For example, the Old Testament has many stories about the Old Covenant; pagan nations practiced blood sacrifices and offering children to their idols. Also, when the Hebrews entered a blood covenant, they would follow a precise ritual in which they exchanged robes and belts, and an animal would be split down the middle and broken in two to make the blood flow. Maybe you learned that Abraham was ready to sacrifice his only son to Yahweh. Instead, he offered a ram caught in nearby bushes."

"Now, the New Testament tells us about the life of Jesus. His passion and death are the embodiment of this 'blood-covenant ritual;' with his blood, Christ washed away our sins. During mass, the initiates partake in the ceremony and symbolically eat his flesh and drink his blood."

What did all this have to do with the ceremony I watched a while ago, I wondered. I was curious where she was going with this.

"What you are trying to tell me is that a ritual where they sacrifice an innocent goat has something to do with the Catholic religion? I don't get it."

"Sure you get it; that's exactly what I'm saying. These Old World rituals have remained in practice today after crossing oceans and surviving unimaginable odds; they have endured the test of time. They speak to Earth's spirits using the primeval language—with elements embedded in the drum vibrations and in the resonances of the languages used in the songs and prayers. They are ingrained, and the frequencies have vibrated with atoms and imprinted psyches for generations."

I then guessed that Toussaint was in this because Grace, his sister, had had a mystical occurrence and not a mysterious disappearance. I was thinking this was crazy but somehow it made sense. We continued our walk on the shoreline toward a rocky peninsula, as my acquaintance explained that many Caribbean people like her inherit beliefs and practices that some may not consider a religion.

We stopped by some dark grey rocks for a moment in silence. The air smelled wet, like it was going to rain soon. Mini shells had colonized the rocks. Looking closely I softly pricked my fingers on their pointy black-and-white portable-homes. At arm's length, they completely blended in with their habitat. The basalt rocks, beaten relentlessly by the waves never softened, not even with time. I marveled at another instance of an amazing occurrence in nature. Paused in thought, I watched a silhouette rise out of the sea.

It had to be Grace; I could tell by her size and proportions, by the way she carried her head and swayed her arms. Then she walked, and I knew that walk. I was blown away and just stared at her come toward us. My numb feet managed to carry me a few steps forward. I could see by now that my senses hadn't betrayed me; my eyes could now make out Grace's face.

"GRACE!" I stumbled forward, banging my toe against a rock.

"CANELA!" her voice cracked. I stopped because of my bleeding toe and she took the few steps that separated us. I was so happy to see my friend! I gave her a super hug and shook her, not believing it could really be her. I held her hands, her shoulders, and then her head; it was Grace!

"GIRL, where the hell have you been?" I was laughing my head off. She looked at me, and then turned her attention to the person by my side.

"Hello," she said, politely tilting her head. Wherever she had been, my girlfriend came back with good manners. I wasn't about to forget mine. I turned around, looking at my helper, and explained that this was my long lost and disappeared friend, Grace. But I didn't know my companion's name, so I couldn't make presentations. I looked hesitant. Grace smiled, telling my lady friend she looked very much like a friend she had recently met.

"Maybe it was my relative, what was her name?"

Grace answered, "Rozalen, what's yours?"

"Believe it or not, my name is also Rozalen. I was named for my aunt, my mom's sister, who disappeared over 21 years ago. Do you think it's possible you saw my aunt? Where did you come from? You just walked out of the ocean!"

We both looked at her, anxious to hear the answer. Instead, she put her hand in her pocket and pulled out a red rock.

"Look my friend, I brought you a present!" Laying flat on the palm of her hand was a broken red disk.

"I thought of you during my journey, which I'll tell you all about as we walk home. Have you seen my family? What's the story since I left?

My eyes were crazy glued to the artifact in her hand. Incredible, it looked just like the one I picked up from the ocean on my way here. I took my part out and put them both together: perfect fit.

It looked like nothing I had ever seen before. Intricately sculpted with designs on the fringe, in the middle was a face with two oval black eyes, a nose with two big nostrils, and a mouth with well-formed and painted teeth. What could it be? A long tongue with a tongue ring hung from the mouth. Between the mouth and the wide nose was a green tube. On both sides of the face in place of ears were round earrings attached to a matching green necklace around the neck. Flaxen hair surrounded the face crowned with a red headband and two green hollow circles at each side of an image; I couldn't make out the designs surrounding the middle.

"Where did you get the other part?" my friend asked amazed.

"That is part is my story after you disappeared."

"Do you girls know what you hold in your hand, Canela?" Rozalen asked.

"I didn't have a clue," I replied.

Grace wondered aloud. "Could it be something from the Indians?"

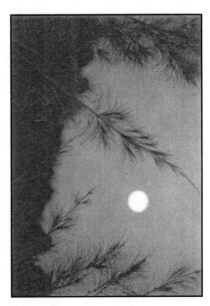

"Good guess, Grace. It's Indian, but not from around here; it comes from Mexico and from a civilization gone before the Aztecs. The artifact in your hand is called the Mayan calendar."

Grace thought about Anacaona and the message she had shared with her.

"Doesn't this tell us about Earth from an astrological perspective? Foretelling planetary events and the like?" Wow, my girlfriend had come back with an "edumacation!" I wondered if she had learned that stuff from under water . . . Rozalen didn't give me a chance to ask my question,

"Modern mankind is still trying to figure out the meaning of this calendar, but it knows one thing for sure."

"And?"

"It is one of the mysteries of our time. Mayans describe the present time as a merging from the dark into the light. They predicted the cycle of light will come in full force on December 21, 2012 and this transition will take us to the cycle of 13 lights and 13 heavens."

"What do you mean, Rozalen?"

"Some believe it will be the birth of a different world and the evolution of mankind into cosmic consciousness."

A new world, really, and in a few years?! I realized that I was going to have to start doing some research to look up this information on the Internet to keep up with my friends . . . The world is changing before us and I, like most of mankind, hadn't even noticed!

ILLUSTRATIONS:

Ch 1. Baron's Cross, Shanik Nouban
Ch 1, Water picture, RoxTaino, Roxane Ledan
Ch 2, Port Salut Island, RoxTaino, Roxane Ledan
Ch 2, Carnival King , Bernard Wah, Roi
Ch 3 Wosh sispann dwarf, Heza Barjon
Ch 5 Ayizan, Heza Barjon
Ch 11 and 12 Olivier Flambert
Ch 17, Pierre, Heza Barjon
Ch 19, Caribbean Ocean, Olivier Flambert
Ch 20, Agwe City, Préfète Duffault
Ch 21, Sunset, RoxTaino, Roxane Ledan
Ch 22, Moon in the pine, RoxTaino, Roxane Ledan
Glossary, Ogou's machete, RoxTaino, Roxane Ledan

All veve designs were provided by Ginette and Daniel Mathurin, many thanks.

GLOSSARY

Agwe: Male vodou archetype master of the seas. Agwe is one of Ezili Freda's husbands, and along with LaSiren, LaBalenn and other watery lwa, represents the great intuitive powers and deep knowledge of the ocean.

Anacaona : Queen of the Taino Xaragua kingdom captured, tortured and murdered by Nicolas Ovando.

Anbadlo: Under water, literally; established place of a parallel spiritual world that are believed to exist under the seas, lakes and rivers.

Ayizan Vélékété : The elder first mambo in Haitian vodou mythology

Ayizan Vélékété, négresse mamou, ladée négresse Fréda Dahomey, négresse fredassy Fréda, négresse flavoum fréda, négresse cissafleur Vodoun da Guinen, kanjole sousafleur Vodu dagimen: sacred prayer in coded language.

Baka(h): An evil spirit

Baron Lakwa: Male vodou archetype, home of the cross.

Baron Samedi: Male vodou archetype known as the graveyard master

Baron Simtye: Male vodou archetype appointed guardian of all the dead.

Bejucos: Taino flower necklace

Bohio: Taino home

Boumbas: Taino word for a big dug out canoe

Cacique: Taino chief

Caonabo : King of the Maguana of Cariban origin

chou-ouek: description of the sound made by the red-legged Thrush

Dahomey Dahomey: was the name of a country in Africa now called the Republic of Benin

Dantò: Feminine angel representing the darker side of Ezili Freda

Deminem Caracol : Half man half turtle; an original among the first of the Taino creation myth.

Duho: Special Taino seat

Ezili (Erzuli): Feminen archetype in Haitian vodou mythology

Fréda : Feminine angel in Haitian vodou mythology represented by a coquettish fair virgin other side of Ezili Danto.

Gwo bonanj: Part of the soul that returns to the collective consciousness

Imamou: Agwe moves with infinite grace and power. His domain is the deep, under currents of the oceans, which he traverses with ease in his boat the Imamou.

Jebourik or waree seed: a round brown seed from the caracole plant and is a counter-poison

Jewouj: Garde of the Ezili nation

Larimar: Larimar (also Lorimar) is a rare blue variety of pectolite found only in the Dominican Republic, in the Caribbean.

Legba : Male archetype in Haitian vodou mythology, he opens the ritual.

Lwa: Angel or spirit belonging to the vodou cosmogony also called mystery.

Mambo : vodou priestess

Mestizo: DNA from different gene pools traditionally categorized as pertaining to race.

Met Agwe! Tawoyo, Koki Lame: Sacred greeting for Agwe

Mystery: Synonym for spirit or angel

Nanm: the spiritual counter part of the body

Nayilé: Female angel name of LaSiren in Agwe's nation

Neg sekle kite, neg kokoye Meye, Neg Oloucoun, Baron and Ghede families: Sacred greeting

Négresse mamou, ladée négresse, négresse fredassy Fréda, négresse flavoum fréda, négresse cissafleur Vodoun dagimen, Kanjole sousafleu vodou dan Guinée: sacred words of the ritual

Nibo: Captain of the vodou Nereids known as the Water Mysteries

Ogu Balendjo, Batioke Nago, Three Islands, and I'm an original Oloukoun: Sacred and code name given to Ogu Balendjo

Palmchat: The Palmchat is the national bird of the Dominican Republic.

Papa Legba, k'ap e pase e e la veye zo: Papa Legba who passes by watch your step

Papa lwa: Respectful name given to a sacred male archetype

Pierre: Male vodou archetype precedes Gede

Pye Danbala: Is another name for Nibo, chief mate of Agwe's fleet

Pitit lakou: People cured by or initiated by the priest or priestess in a lakou or family neighborhood

Portolano maps: a descriptive atlas of the Middle Ages, giving sailing directions and providing charts showing rhumb lines and the location of ports and various coastal features.

Rara(h): Neighborhood or group dancing band in Haiti

Savalwe: Traditional greeting

Ti bonanj: In vodou, considered part of the soul that is personal

tic tic tic: Description of the sound made by the Hispaniolan Emerald

toca-loro: description of the sound made by the Hispaniolan Trogon

Veve: sacred vodou designs

Waree seed: Mucuna fawcettii. Caribbean drift seed. Hilum thicker than other Mucuna species.

Wosh Sispann: A rock energized by a sorcerer with the breath of a dying person.

Yayayel: The first turtle who gave birth to Deminem Cararcol, half man half turtle, in the Taino creation myth

CHAPTER 18 ENDNOTES

1. Check out that fine hussy.
2. I know you have a big (explicit sexual word referring to male genitalia) that can (explicit verb referring to a sexual act) this woman's (explicit term referring to a woman's genitalia).
3. I'm taking you to my dad, I know he will be (explicit sexual term meaning aroused) when he sees (vulgar term for breasts) on the babe you are walking with.
4. So who's the twerp? Your son?
5. Want a shot of fire (to your explicit term meaning genitals) my prince?
6. Oh damn, look at that guy drinking the hot booze, man you are incredible!
7. To hell with them all, my booze is finished.

AUTHOR BIO

Geneviève Douyon Flambert is a Haitian-American educator born and raised in the USA, who embraced a Caribbean reality the second half of her life. Writing provides insights in determining her identity, immersed in the on-going process of acquiring languages and accepting cultures. The author is fluent in four Caribbean languages, Spanish, English, French and Creole and tries to use each one in her writing, to express perceptions and representations unique to that part of the world where reality has been described as more incredible than fiction. Geneviève lives with her family on the two-nation island once called Kiskeya.

http://caribanstories.com

http://2012on1221.wordpress.com

http://hubpages.com/profile/OnaCaribbeanVibe

LaVergne, TN USA
23 November 2009
165051LV00002B/3/P